Jottings

LIZ SMITH

Jottings

Flights of Fancy from Our Betty

With illustrations
by the author

POCKET
BOOKS

LONDON • SYDNEY • NEW YORK • TORONTO

First published in Great Britain by Simon & Schuster UK Ltd, 2007
This edition first published by Pocket Books, 2008
An imprint of Simon & Schuster UK Ltd
A CBS COMPANY

3 5 7 9 10 8 6 4 2

Simon & Schuster UK Ltd
1st Floor
222 Gray's Inn Road
London WC1X 8HB

www.simonsays.co.uk

Simon & Schuster Australia
Sydney

A CIP catalogue record for this book is available
from the British Library

ISBN: 978-1-84739-165-0

Typeset in Palatino by M Rules
Printed by CPI Cox & Wyman, Reading, Berkshire RG1 8EX

Contents

Introduction

I have written these stories over many years. Each one has been sparked off by a memory which has gathered thoughts around it until it became something I wanted to write down.

For instance, the story of Eliza came from the time I worked at the National Theatre in *When We Are Married* by J.B. Priestley.

I played the part of the charwoman, Mrs Eliza Northrop, who just came into the house to do all the dirty jobs and got the sack by the end of the play. Well, I used to sit in the wings waiting for my cue, and in my mind went home with Mrs Northrop, and it was awful: a truly wretched experience. A foul, damp dwelling to live in and a foul, violent husband to live with. She was middle-aged, which in those days was old.

I thought, I will alter your life, Eliza. I will make something happen that will change your life and you will have a new beginning, in the same way that my own life altered from that age. So in the story, she goes to the party, as it is in the play, and then something happens off stage. From that moment, she has a life she never dreamed of.

A world away from J.B. Priestley in 1908 came the idea for 'The Stockings', set in the desolate landscape of 1934. That was when I was a child, wandering around the countryside on my bicycle. An opening in a scraggy hedge led into a cart rut which had shaped itself into a dragon, so the village was called Dragonby. The entire village consisted of only two joined cottages, standing beside a stagnant pond. When I was peddalling along the nearly empty roads, I never saw the people who lived there but I stood long, with my bicycle, thinking what their lives would be like. No bus service to town, only candles and oil lamps, life rough and crude like an early Van Gogh painting.

It would be another forty years before I wrote about the place, but the feelings of desolation were as strong then as they were when I stood at the gap in the hedge.

So it goes on.

'The Kid' started at a time when I had small grand-children and learned a lot about nannies. How they banded together in groups, raided the fridges, swapped charges and toured the world, meeting up on another continent.

The girl in the flat upstairs had a baby and I used to

watch the nanny pushing the pram up the road and wonder where she would take it for a whole day, so the mother could go to the gym and then lunch with a friend.

Impressions stay, like the flash of a camera. As for the time they take to develop, well, it does not seem to matter.

Monologue over a Broken Leg

'I don't know what it is about him, but he made me burn the moment I clapped eyes on him.'

The eyes appeared occasionally over the vast expanse of plaster, the voice boomed over the white mountain.

Sue had to lie still because the stitches were new. She was bound tightly to her bed with crisp white sheets, so, with half-closed eyes, she listened.

'Don't get the idea that he's a husky film-star type, rippling muscles and all that. No, as a matter of fact he's a bit weedy, and his colour's not all that good you know. I think it's all those trips abroad and he's had fever once or twice. Don't know what fever exactly, some local bug, not serious, but it leaves one like a limp rag.

'Poor darling, he told me how absolutely bloody he'd felt lying there all day in this bungalow place where they live out there. The rest of them simply had to go out and get on with the job, well, the Min. of Ag. wanted all these details about trees and grasses and whatnot and as they were footing the bill they jolly well had to have them.

'So, of course the poor darling had to be left alone while the others got on with the tree marking and whatnot, except for native servants – they brought him cool drinks and so forth.

'The outcome of all this was that he was a bit under the weather after this trip and he had very little to say for himself when I went to tea with his mother. Have I mentioned her teas before? Stop me if I have, but they're traditional, absolutely trad, my dear. The lot. Old silver, been in the family for yonks, minute but min*ute* sandwiches – practically lose them in my great paws.

'Look, they *are* great paws, aren't they? They have to be, a mobile library takes a bit of holding round these country lanes, you know.

'But to get back to Ronnie, or rather, the first time I ever met him, well, as I said, his mother was pouring tea and nattering on fifteen to the dozen as is her wont, and the poor dear just grabbed the opportunity to slide down into the armchair and practically disappear. All I could see was a shaft of sunlight streaming through the French windows and shining on his nearly bald head under a thin layer of hair, pale hair, you know, an indifferent shade of mouse, and of course, I must admit, it didn't go with his complexion which was a bit yellow at the time, after-effects of fever and all that.

'And that was the first thing that got me here, just here.' She beat her barrel-like chest with a mighty thud. 'It was somehow so pathetic, so revealing, like a secret that had to be told. I could see he was bald under the hair he pulled over. It touched me.

'Well, of course I grabbed him out of the chair as soon as I decently could. He said no no no he hated tennis but I yanked him out, told him he needed a spot of fresh air. I knew he'd relax pretty quickly as soon as I got him away from his mama.

'And by golly he did. Before I could get the rackets sorted out, he was off, full pelt, on his favourite subject: bird and insect life in Africa.

'Mama still seemed to be pouring tea and going on about her favourite subjects, usually centred around the Women's Institute. I could hear her voice droning through the open window like an old gramophone stuck in the groove.

'So I just threw the rackets down on the floor of the summer house and gave myself up to ecstasy. I just sat on the bench and listened to Ronnie without hearing a word he said. I felt better sitting down because I'm just a little bit taller you know, I'm . . . well, let's face it, I'm a big girl.

'Perhaps it was partly this bigness of mine and Ronnie

being a bit on the small side that gave me this protective feeling towards him. Protect him? . . . I wanted to smother him. I wanted to wrap my arms around him so tightly that he screamed for help and then I wanted to close his screaming mouth with kisses. Yes! That was the effect he had on me right from the start. I knew I wanted him and I was determined to have him.

'I was so excited by the discovery that I got my new tweed skirt stuck in the spokes, wobbled too much on the old bike on me way home. I could hardly sleep that night and the next day I stamped the wrong date on three separate books.

'I did worse things the following day, which was Tuesday. On Tuesdays, you see, I always take the library to Wilford. Instead of that, I drove straight on to Burford. You should have seen the uproar THAT caused. It was market day. I landed right in the middle of it and the poor souls just gaped at me with their mouths hanging open. They were frozen, didn't know whether to carry on filling their baskets at the stalls or dash home and get their library books to change.

'I saw several decide to do both and walk back and forth in an aimless sort of way before they set in their tracks and just stood gawking helplessly. It would take weeks to recover their sense of rhythm and they would probably never feel the same about me again, so I decided I had to do something about it. I had to see him again to see if my first feelings still existed or if I had just been under some strange midsummer madness.

'I called at the house that evening. He was mounting beetle specimens onto a sheet of blue paper, his head was bent and the lamplight caught his spectacles – they're rather thick you know, his glasses, he's a bit short-sighted – but as I said, the lamplight just glowed through the lens and my heart went so thick with emotion I could hardly speak. I just stood there staring at him, and he went on, carefully arranging his beetles.

'His mother didn't seem to notice a thing, she was pouring something, coffee, or maybe cocoa, and talking on and on as usual about Mrs Somebody-or-other at the Women's Institute.

'The feelings I experienced that night were confirmed on the Thursday when I went to Melford.

'Now, library day in Melford is every other Thursday and our spot there is outside the Carpenter's Arms. So, as total silence descends on the place between two and three o'clock, I always nip in for a quick one before closing time and as the bolts are thrown across, I remain inside, then retire, inflamed by half a pint of bitter, to spend a lusty half hour with Fred, who's the barman there. The landlord retires to his own quarters to snore away for an hour or two and Fred's room is conveniently

situated over the stables down the yard, so we can romp in peace.

'And romp we did. A well-made country boy is Fred, and I always came away from library day in Melford with a feeling of immense satisfaction.

'But that day, the Thursday after the Tuesday when I had seen Ronnie, I didn't want Fred. I didn't want him. He couldn't believe it. I walked out of the door before he shot the bolt, and he nearly cried with disappointment. All the rest of the afternoon, I could see his big sad eyes peering at me through the letter T on the frosted glass window. I was glad to get away, I can tell you.

'All I could think about was Ronnie, he was burning me up.

'It was the same on the following Wednesday when I went to Trill. Trill has a library every Wednesday, and by Linton crossroads there's a dirty great barn. Perhaps you've noticed it? Used to belong to Frank Johnstone when he farmed around there. Been empty for years, practically derelict now, filthy of course but still quite a bit of hay in the loft there.

'Well, I used to stop there and by the time I'd smoked a cigarette, John Forman would arrive too. John drives for Carter's the butchers, he does all the country districts and we've had this arrangement for years. It didn't matter who got there first. You can imagine, we were there, the hay was there, so we had a roll in the hay. Every Wednesday.

'But this Wednesday, the one following the Tuesday when I'd seen the old darling, I drove straight past the barn. I did. I drove straight past the barn and John was already there. His van was standing, drawn up to the barn and he was leaning out of the gaping windows. I can see him now, first of all looking anxious as I didn't slow down, then shouting and waving after me as I didn't stop.

'But I couldn't help myself. I drove those books as if I was carrying a banner. I WAS carrying a banner. I was saving myself for Ronnie.

'Of course, I couldn't go the whole hog right away and as I built up my visits to his mother, so I cut down to only seeing Jack Clymie after choir practice. We had an arrangement to stay behind, put the books away, pick the chewing gum off the pews, etcetera, etcetera.

'You wouldn't think Jack was sexy, would you? My God! What goes on behind that saturnine countenance and those hooded eyes is just nobody's business, a whiplash of cool steely passion is our Jack. But gradually, even he became impossible because, as we cavorted in our favourite spot, which was in the hollow behind 'Lady Abigail Flower, gud wife and mother of fourteen', where she has lain stonily since sixteen something, and where I was laid, non-stonily, once a week, I looked up from my position on my back into the vaulted roof and saw the little cherub faces peering down at me from the tops of the columns. They were all little Ronnies! In the dim light I fancied they were all wearing specs.

'No, I decided, this was it. This is where I just stopped and waited, let passion snowball to explode over the little love in a shower of hot snowflakes, so to speak.

'He was due back from some remote jungle in South America in about twelve weeks. The whole thing became an obsession. I was determined to make the plan and just go ahead with it. Now, Nick Thompson has a caravan down by the river at Whaley. Had it for years, used to do quite a bit of fishing until rheumatism got him. He lets it when he's in the mood and it's in a pretty remote place, I can tell you. It's thick with bugs, beetles, flies and what-not down there, so the prospect of all that would keep the little darling happy.

'I'd been down to check over the caravan. It smelled a bit stale and mouldy so I'd aired it and made the bed up nice and comfy. Then I just went around in a dream, slapping on the old date stamp, and waiting for his return.

'I picked him up at the station. He was standing by a mountain of assorted boxes with mysterious bug-type labels and his glasses had never looked thicker. I could

The little darling with Fred, his
favourite spider.

have eaten him. I felt like placing him tenderly into one of his specimen jars and just gazing at him.

'I don't think he noticed when I told him of the trip I planned for the weekend, as he was watching a spider at the time and just kept on nodding, so I told him I'd pick him up on Thursday evening. His mother didn't even realize he was going away for the weekend, she was chattering on about the church fête and pouring endless cups of tea or coffee.

'Believe it or not, the great day came. The weather was wonderful. The river was shimmering and alive with flies. The scene was set for a heavenly weekend. Little darling was a bit preoccupied as we drove down there. The string had worked loose on one of his boxes. In fact he nearly dropped it when he got out of the van. I leaped forward and grabbed it for him. Well, I grabbed the box, and then, quite instinctively, I grabbed him. It seemed the right thing to do, to carry the beloved aloft, over the threshold of our bedchamber in the traditional way. In a great surge of emotion I swept him up in my arms and mounted the steps of the caravan.

'We were on the top step when they gave way. Just a loud sharp noise. CRACK. That was the step. Followed by another loud sharp noise. CRACK. That was my leg.

'Oh God! I hope I'm mobile by the time he comes back again.'

Fog

London, 1953

One experience never to be forgotten about life in London during the 1940s and 50s was the fog. Not the pale mist that crept around the trees at dawn in a wild garden, but a menacing vapour of darkness that smelled of soot and obscured anything beyond the tip of your nose.

At that time, no one I knew had central heating and we all piled coal merrily on the fire. My coal was kept in a cupboard halfway up the house. It would arrive in sacks on a cart drawn by a great horse, then was hauled up the stairs by a giant of a man and dumped onto the floor. It took a while for the dust to settle. But the coal was of excellent quality and shone like diamonds.

We saved the tea leaves to dampen down the fire when we went to bed. When my son was born, the midwife stoked up the fire, rolled up the afterbirth in newspaper and pushed it into the hot coals.

FoG 1953

The greatest fog experience I can remember was in 1953. Then, the black darkness refused to stay outside in the streets and down the alleyways, but invaded us completely, and took over our homes, shops and pubs – every space you can think of.

Everywhere inside was filled with this thick, black mist. We could scarcely see one another in the floating darkness because lights shone dimly as if far away. Out in the streets, lights did not show at all. There was just a wall of black. You were afraid to put one foot in front of the other.

One couple I heard of were standing in the street, paralysed, rigid, unable to move an inch as the darkness was so solid around them. Out of the black came footsteps and a man's voice asked them where they wished to go. They told him the address and he said to hang onto his jacket and he would take them there, which he did. When they were feeling their way into their own front door, they asked him how he had managed it.

'Well, you see,' he said, 'I am blind, so the fog makes no difference to me.'

Another outcome of the fog getting inside was to do with the shops. We had so many wonderful department stores in those days and after the fogs they had amazing sales of blackened goods. Expensive coats, beautiful dresses, all going for next to nothing because there was a line of soot running from top to bottom

Then came the Clean Air Act of 1956.

The Kid

Pamela squashed a Weetabix in a bowl and gave it to the kid. She shouldn't be doing it anyway, but no sign of Gerda yet.

The kid spilled the cereal onto the floor and the sight of the sticky mess irritated Pamela out of all proportion. It spoiled her kitchen. Pamela was prepared, and in fact, often did, move a saucer from one end to the other, simply to pause, narrow her eyes, tilt her head and look for camera angles.

Click. That would show the beauty of the Italian furniture.

Click, in this picture the Wedgwood china would show and maybe a little of the conservatory beyond.

Click, click and click again as the conservatory came fully into sight. Black and white tiled floor. White enamelled bamboo furniture, a mass of potted palms, and to her endless delight, a life-sized statue of Pan. She had found him in a shop near Selfridge's. A shop that had once catered for the extravagant tastes of the oil sheiks. When the oil sheiks no longer came, Pan was on sale for a fraction of his original price and was quickly transferred to Pamela's conservatory where his mischievous face of white and gold china peered through the palms.

Standing near the doorway, Pamela's eyes scanned as a camera lens down the whole vista of her beautiful kitchen where across the gleaming floor ran the trickle of sticky milk and crushed biscuit. It offended her.

Click, went her eye.

Even the kid herself spoiled the pattern, sitting in the high chair in front of the pale ash, designer-built cupboards. She would make sure the high chair was well out of the way if *Ideal Home* ever did feature her kitchen. Surely, one day they would.

As she cleaned up the mess, Pamela heard the dull thud of Gerda on the stairs. Her steps were slow and heavy, signalling another hangover. Pamela looked up as she polished the floor and saw Gerda's feet advancing towards her. Minnie Mouse boots, she noticed, and wondered what the rest of her was wearing today.

Looking up, she saw brief shorts with a Union Jack on the behind, a jacket of many colours, and a peaked cap, no doubt concealing uncombed hair.

Gerda gently lowered herself onto a stool. 'You hev

coffee?' she said, holding her head carefully between her hands.

'Help yourself. Not feeling too good?'

'You could say that, ya. I am not feeling up to eet today, but I will recover,' she said bravely. 'I want to take de kid to de zoo. I weel have de seltzer for breakfast and all weel be well.'

Pamela hovered over the breadboard, knife in hand. 'Toast?' she said.

'Oh God. De idea of food eet makes me feel so bad,' and Gerda exhaled a blast of stale wine fumes.

What a repellent picture, thought Pamela, and her camera eye went click. That picture would look good in the alternative *Ideal Home*, exquisite kitchen defiled by sight of nanny, still drunk from last night's disco orgy. Face blotched, eyes bleary, begging for seltzer.

'I'm afraid there's no seltzer, Gerda. You've used them all up.'

Pamela dug the knife into the loaf and pretended it was Gerda. Gerda, she called herself, what was her real name? Probably something like Sharon or Helen, and as for that stupid accent, well, why did she have to do it? It altered from day to day. Did the stupid girl think she would get a better job with an accent? It was obvious from the ill-written letters she received that she came from Cleethorpes. Why pretend Cleethorpes was in Sweden?

Pamela made the loaf suffer. She cut so hard the crust fell off. 'Gerda, if you are going to the zoo, buy some more bread, and stick it in the freezer. I notice the pizzas have gone and most of the ice cream. You'd better buy more of everything. Were the girls here yesterday?'

'Ya they came round, we had little play together, the kid had good time, company you know.'

'They can certainly eat,' said Pamela as she put money on the table. 'Do the other houses provide so much?'

'Some more,' said Gerda with a leer. 'Kids they play, they get hungry you know.'

To say nothing of the nannies, said Pamela quietly to herself, suddenly wanting them to go and leave her to get on with her day.

Finally, the door clicked behind them and she was alone with a fresh cup of coffee and the call-in programme on the radio. She unfolded her arms above her head like a cat. What bliss, all the day stretched out before her. She could do exactly as she wished.

On the radio, worried voices were explaining to a financial expert how they could not pay their bills. The expert explained in soothing tones how they must do this or do that to get out of the mess.

Poor sods, thought Pamela. You'd better give up now. You can't win. You're losers. Almost instinctively, she drew her handbag towards her and checked her credit cards were in place. Whatever else I do today, she decided, I'll spend a lot of money.

She stood, letting her white silk dressing gown fall to the floor for the cleaner to pick up and walked naked up the stairs to her room.

She watched her reflection in the mirrored doors of the built-in wardrobe which ran along the length of two walls. She could stand in the angle of the mirrors and see a complete picture of herself, and what she saw pleased her: deep creamy carpet, windows veiled with finest net which drifted across the floor. A dais held her huge bed with the ivory satin sheets and quilt of imitation white fur. By the window stood a white and gold china stand and bowl filled with a huge arrangement of silk flowers. She had found this in the shop with Pan and could not resist buying it together with the flight of birds suspended from the ceiling as if flying out of the flowers.

What a beautiful nest, thought Pamela. Her room was a dream. How lucky she was to have a friend like Tony, an interior decorator, to turn to for advice. Tony was such an understanding person who never designed a room without first consulting the relevant birth charts.

'Your star sign says you must live with gentle colours in peace,' he had told her.

'I know, Tony, I know. That's the kind of room I want

21

for myself, but how can I achieve it with a slob of a husband like Bernard?'

'There's no doubt, duckie,' replied Tony, 'that the idiot doesn't reflect your psyche. He just doesn't complement you, luvvie.'

Pamela raised her eyebrows in exasperation. 'I just don't need him,' she said.

'You need his money,' said Tony, who in spite of his extravagant lifestyle was a practical man at heart.

'Alas, yes, I do.'

'How does he make so much just selling glass?'

'It isn't called magic glass for nothing you know, it's self cleaning, a secret formula. Just think what it means to the builders of glass skyscrapers in cities like Los Angeles. They buy it by the ton and he's the only representative of the firm. He doesn't even have to try to sell it; they're lining up with orders. If he had to make any effort himself he'd be penniless, he's so stupid. He didn't even get the job himself, his uncle wangled it for him.'

'There's only one answer, luvvie,' said Tony. 'A separate room.'

'Brilliant,' said Pamela. 'But how?'

It had been effortless. Simply announcing he was too restless in his sleep and kept her awake, she dismissed Bernard to the room at the end of the corridor.

Pamela and Tony had had a glorious time in Knightsbridge finding exactly the right stuff for her room. It had even included a visit to a reader of stones and crystals to make sure they were on the right track. The result was a triumph.

Dear Tony, thought Pamela, I wonder if he's free for lunch, and she picked up the phone. He told her he would love to meet but had to leave early for an appointment.

She had to look her best, as Tony noted precisely what she wore. Delving into the cupboards, she flung clothes around the room. Finally, she chose a two-piece of the softest pale-blue wool. When she opened the blouse cupboard, the first thing she touched was Daddy's dressing gown. She stood inside the cupboard and wrapped it around her. She smelled it, pressing it to her face. The scent of his tobacco lingered there, a faint touch of his aftershave. She passionately kissed the empty sleeve from top to bottom.

Dearest Daddy. Beloved Daddy. Why had he eaten shellfish in Morocco? To think he had been taken from her by a prawn.

But, for the moment, she needed to focus on what blouse to wear. Nothing seemed right. The only one exciting enough was the Italian silk, of such an exquisite tangle of colour Daddy could easily have brought it

23

back from a trip to Rome. Yes, no doubt, it was her most beautiful blouse. She had to wear it today. She knew Tony would approve.

Pamela wiped a brush over her lipstick and carefully outlined her mouth.

In an odd kind of way it would be an added excitement to wear the blouse knowing that she had stolen it. She had stolen it from Maureen Bell at the health club. Maureen had booked in for an hour's massage. There had been no one else in the changing rooms and Pamela had a long time to inspect the lockers. It was just a little habit she had, it was quite harmless. If anyone was stupid enough to leave their door unlocked when they went for a swim they had to expect someone would have a peek at their belongings.

She enjoyed finding cheap underwear under an Ungaro suit, she loved finding a love letter or a final demand for rent; she had gone through people's stuff many times before just for the thrill of it but had never stolen anything.

Until she had opened Maureen's locker.

She had known Maureen almost all of her life. They were at kindergarten together, then right through school until they were eighteen.

Maureen Bell was the dullest creature she had ever known. From day one at kindergarten she had used the stupid creature as a whipping donkey. As a small child she had made her suffer mental torture. Poor little Maureen had endured months of agony having been told that there was a lion in her toy cupboard, a snake in her pyjamas, spiders in her bedtime cocoa. Her mother couldn't understand why she did not drink it.

And so it went on, right through school. As they grew older, the cruelties became more subtle, and more painful. Her long hair trapped in the cloakroom door did not leave a mark. To be locked in the bike shed until after roll-call only brought down the wrath of the head-mistress.

It was easy to be angry with Maureen, it was easy to shout, because she didn't retaliate. She was so plain. A plump child, with mousey hair and ill-shaped teeth. She invited abuse because she responded only with silent acceptance.

As she grew plainer so Pamela grew prettier. As Pamela's attacks became meaner and stronger, so Maureen's offer of a truce became more frequent. Chocolates, stockings, even cigarettes were slyly passed in the playground, desperate to find favour.

Well, all that was a long time ago, and now Maureen was a very unattractive woman indeed. So what did she want with a blouse like this? thought Pamela.

The silk had slipped through Pamela's fingers like

water. She had hesitated just a second before she tried it on. God! She looked beautiful in it. The dazzling colours made her golden hair look like the sun, flattered her complexion so that she glowed. She preened in front of the mirror. It just did not seem right that this beautiful thing belonged to a dreary inspector of taxes. It was ridiculous. On her, it was in its rightful place. If Maureen could but see her in it she would agree; she would press her to take it as she had pressed the toffees on her long ago. The blouse just was not Maureen's style.

By the time Pamela folded it and packed it into her own bag she had persuaded herself that she was doing Maureen a favour.

Pamela picked up her bag in the kitchen and as she waited for her taxi she polished the golden horns on the white china face of Pan, kissing his leering lips before she left.

❦

Gerda had known in her bones that today wasn't going to be a good day. She really had meant that the kid would go to the zoo, but not necessarily that she would take her herself. The gang would always help out.

The gang was grouped around the gates at the zoo when she arrived: Sally, Karen, Pat. Gerda made the fourth member. A tight little group, they had been together for several years in a completely unattached way. The four girls nannied their way around the world, and always drifted in the same direction.

They met up in Hong Kong, in Africa, in America and formed exactly the same group. Because of their close understanding of one another they could sit together wordless in Melbourne or Muswell Hill.

They shifted their jobs frequently, sometimes to get a different postal address, sometimes for a new swimming pool, and always passionately loved the child they had just left. Their charges became a playgroup and they swapped the caring from one to another using bed and board within their circle.

No trouble, decided Gerda, the kid would be cared for by the gang. They would take her around the zoo with them, then go back with one of them to sleep, until Gerda was back from her date.

The girls stood beside their cars in a bunch. An irritating wind had sprung up bringing a few spots of rain.

Karen swept a heap of cigarette ends from her car into the gutter. She was pale from the night before. 'Pissing awful day,' she said. 'I hate the zoo when it rains.'

'So do I,' said Sally. 'It's bad enough on a good day. I feel so sorry for 'em when it's cold weather.'

'Especially the big monkeys,' said Karen.

'Well, that's a good start,' said Gerda. 'OK if I leave the kid with you?'

'Aw heck, my headache's killing me,' said Karen. 'And we're overloaded already.'

Gerda peered into the cars. 'Martin and David, why are they here?'

'Shirley's not well, and we owe her a day anyway.'

The idea slowly dawned on Gerda that she might have to take the kid with her. She kicked the edge of the pavement for a while, her arms twisted behind her back, scowling at her friends. They had become oddly silent and were not in the mood to be persuaded. They knew she was going to meet Eric and were trying to make her change her mind.

The girls moved towards their cars and started strapping their charges into pushchairs. Gerda walked to her car as slowly as she could hoping they would recall her, but they didn't. She sat in her driver's seat for a long time, watching as they assembled and walked towards the zoo entrance. As they went through the gate, only Sally turned and waved her a brief salute.

She sat, biting her fingernails watching the space they had left. Spots of rain appeared on her windscreen. She had no choice. She had to take the kid with her. She slowly nosed her car around the park and emerged into Regent Street, from there, she turned into Soho.

❀

Pamela walked down Sloane Street and wished she lived in Knightsbridge. She always had the same thoughts whenever she was shopping there. She wanted to live where she could pop into Harrods food department daily. Wander around. Buy a delicious morsel here, an unusual parcel of food there, take it home, serve it on an exquisite tablecloth – pink or maybe daring navy blue.

Of course, she would fill up the nanny's fridge with food from Sainsbury's. Where was the Sainsbury's in Knightsbridge? Pamela mused, as she gazed into the shop windows.

She had a coffee in the General Trading Co., and a chocolate slice that exploded hundreds of calories over her taste buds. Delicious, she thought. So civilized. She belonged here.

She chose some cutlery and ordered two large flower pots for the garden. The customer standing by her who gave her name and address to the assistant had a title. Pamela was purring with satisfaction when she handed over her credit card.

In the street, a nasty little wind whipped her hair and shed a few spots of rain, but she scarcely noticed.

She stopped at an art gallery. Interesting. A tall elegant girl watched her from the desk inside the shop. She would go in; she didn't want that girl to think she wasn't used to art galleries. Even to buying art.

The paintings were very large. They had very little on them. A line here, a circle there. She stopped in front of one huge canvas which was completely black with just a tiny crimson spot in the lower corner. There was a green scrawl but that seemed to be the artist's name.

'Stunning isn't it,' drawled the tall girl.

'Stunning,' reiterated Pamela.

'Do you collect him?' said the girl.

'Not yet,' replied Pamela. 'But I may start.'

'You should,' advised the guardian of the gallery, lowering her shell-like eyelids. 'I'll give you a hot tip – buy now. We're selling them at a giveaway price. This time next year they will have doubled, trebled in value.'

'What is the price of this one?' enquired Pamela.

'Thirty-five thousand.'

'Oh.'

'This time next year you can add on another hundred thou.' The sage nodded solemnly.

Pamela nodded knowingly in return and backed out of the door with a murmured 'thank you'.

She went to MaxMara and bought a skirt. She felt she had a bargain, as that too was a work of art. She bought shoes in Harrods, two outfits for the kid, then plunged into Harvey Nichols.

She was deep in discussion with a helpful attendant, trying to decide between a white silk two-piece and a pale lemon trouser suit, when Tony appeared.

'How did you find me?' she cried.

'I was working just around the corner, and I knew instinctively that you were here,' he said as he dropped a butterfly kiss on each cheek.

'You looked in your crystal,' she cried with a laugh that was a little too shrill.

'I knew you needed me.'

'I do need you desperately. Which one is it to be, the yellow or the white?'

She paraded the two outfits for him, and he was quite definite. 'Both,' he said.

So she bought both.

She handed her card to the girl and noted she was suitably impressed with Tony. He looked so handsome this morning in a silver grey designer suit with a lilac striped shirt. His hair was just going silver at the temples, and Pamela thought how well it matched his suit.

How lucky she was to have him for a friend. What a social asset he was. Imagine if she had come shopping with Bernard, what an embarrassment that would have been. He would be chewing his nails, shifting his feet and causing her so much anxiety that she would hardly be able to acknowledge him. Of course, he wouldn't have a clue which garment suited her. He had no sense of style.

They took a taxi to Luigi's. Pamela watched Tony over her pile of parcels.

'You were working around the corner?' she enquired.

'Yes, my sweet, but I can't say where.' He touched his lips with his forefinger. ''Fraid it's on the secret list.'

'Not, not one of the Royals?' Her eyes widened.

'Say no more, but you could be getting warm,' and he patted her knee.

Pamela leaned back in the taxi and glowed. What a lucky girl she was. She had a house fit for an article in *Ideal Home* and a friend like Tony. A friend who was stylish enough to escort her anywhere, and was a joy to be with. So witty. So amusing. So appreciative of all things beautiful. And yet, at the end of the day he went home to his friend Rupert. A kiss on the cheek from Tony meant a kiss on the cheek from Tony. It left her feeling calm and serene.

Luigi stacked her parcels behind the desk and showed them to the table in the centre of the packed and popular restaurant. 'I will care for your parcels,' he said, his Scouse accent heavily overlaid with Italian. Luigi found the accent a bit tiresome at times but he knew it was good for trade and matched the pasta.

He placed the chair tenderly under Pamela. As she sat down his hand brushed her jacket and she cringed.

'Oh Madame,' he cried. 'You are just the tiniest bit damp. You must not chill, we must dry your jacket.'

Without more ado he dragged the jacket from her shoulders, putting it on the back of the chair.

'Very sensible,' said Tony. 'And now I can see your lovely blouse better. The colours are glorious. It's got to be Italian, surely. Such style.'

'From Rome,' lied Pamela. 'One of Daddy's trips.'

'You miss him.'

'Terribly. Terribly.'

Tony ordered melon and Parma ham.

'I did say I'll have to leave early, didn't I, darling?' he said.

'Yes, you did.'

'This will do me nicely until dinner time.'

'I don't want to eat a lot either,' said Pamela. She ordered a grilled salmon steak on a bed of spinach. 'Shall we share a bottle of dry white?'

'Yes.'

'Do you ever come here with your current client? Or do you go to the Ritz or San Lorenzo?'

'No, she really likes it here.'

'Is she frightfully important?'

'Important enough to have a bodyguard.'

'Wow,' said Pamela. 'I bet the rooms you design for her are exquisite.'

'Nothing more beautiful than your own little nest, my sweet.'

Pamela lifted her glass and her eyes gleamed over the rim. At that moment, apart from not living in Knightsbridge, she felt her life was almost perfect.

⚘

Gerda sat fuming in the traffic jam outside the BBC. Slowly she edged towards Oxford Circus, then turned a little too carelessly past Liberty's into Soho. She edged the car past the stalls, sliding over the plastic bags spilling their rotting contents. The disturbed pigeons flew clumsily away.

The video shop where Eric worked had all the latest releases in the window. Those at the back of the shop were not advertised. He was standing at the door talking between little gasps of laughter into the ear of a hugely fat man with a dangerously red face. He was gesticulating and occasionally tapping the man's fat arm. He found the whole story very funny and his long hands flapped about as if they were detaching from his arms.

Eric was a very long person. Long and thin. He had greasy, black hair hanging in an untidy mess, and deep lines running down his thin face making him look older than his years.

He looked up and saw Gerda in her car. He waved his

hands towards her like a broken windmill, then gave the fat man a final tap pushing himself across the pavement. He leaned through the window and handed Gerda a key.

'Sorry about this,' she said.

'What?'

'This, the kid. Had to bring her, they wouldn't have her.' She inclined her head towards the kid strapped into the back seat.

'Hello kid,' said Eric.

The kid looked back with solemn eyes.

'Doesn't laugh much, does she?'

'She's very serious, takes it all in though.'

'Does she talk a lot?'

'No, she can't talk yet.'

'Well, we're all right then, aren't we? She won't tell a soul, and I like a bit of an audience. Couldn't be better. You go on. See you in a minute.'

Gerda took the key and manoeuvred the car past more stalls, round the corner and into the Dickensian court where Eric lived.

The doorway to his room was between a strip shop and a kebab parlour. The sickening smell from the huge wedge-shaped piece of meat filled the little court. Eric looked at the rotating anonymous greasy mess with revulsion every time he approached his door. Eric was a vegetarian.

A man stood in the strip-shop doorway. A vast man of Eastern origin. He stood like a statue, absolutely still, illuminated in flashes by the raw light bulbs around the doorway. He might not have seen her, but Gerda saw the crocodile blink of his heavy-lidded eyes, and she wondered just how many girls he had observed going through Eric's paint-blistered door.

Outside the kebab shop a man wearing several ragged overcoats lay asleep on the pavement. His head rested on several bags from Marks & Spencer, stuffed with more rags and bottles. An empty bottle stood in his sleep-limp hand, urine soaked his trousers and ran down the pavement.

At the creak of the ancient door the man opened his eyes, and looked up at Gerda through a tangle of filthy, matted hair. 'Giv' us some money,' he said. 'Giv' us some money for a cuppa tea.'

Gerda shuddered her way up the narrow, creaking staircase with the kid in her arms, and wished she didn't find Eric so fascinating.

The door to his bed-cum-sitting room stood open and the thin light leaked through the tiny windows. Specs of dust floated in a pale ray of sunshine. Gerda picked her way through the litter of dirty underclothes and T-shirts under her feet.

She lifted the end of the sofa and slipped the kid's

reins under the foot. A few girlie magazines slipped onto the floor. The kid tried to hold one, but Gerda saw the amount of dried tomato juice with clusters of hard, fossilized pips, and thought not. Eric was very fond of tomatoes.

The kid leaned back against the sofa and gazed at her with sad dark eyes.

Gerda thought she might clear up the mess in the sink, but after moving one sticky saucer from one side to another, decided against it. She wandered restlessly towards the bed; the cheap, wine-coloured sheets violently patterned in black and white were in total disarray. She straightened one corner and then thought, what the hell. She sat on the bed and stared at the kid, who stared back at her with brooding eyes.

Eric came bounding up the stairs carrying a DVD in a plain wrapper. 'This one is sensational,' he cried. 'It's murder, plus, plus extra plus.'

He swept back his long greasy hair excitedly as he fixed the DVD in the machine.

When Gerda slipped her clothes off, she turned away from the kid, feeling suddenly embarrassed.

Eric screamed, as usual, at his climax, and the kid cried a lot.

'Tie me up,' said Eric, 'and we'll watch the DVD again.'

Gerda firmly tied his wrists and ankles to the bed with

an assortment of laddered tights. Then she made some tea, and with the last slice of bread, she made some tomato sandwiches and fed them to Eric.

His hands and feet secured to the bed, he watched the DVD, contentedly munching. He drank his tea through a straw and Gerda wiped his mouth with a corner of the sheet. He grinned at her.

'Tomatoes were good,' he said.

'Must be Dutch.'

The DVD ended and she untied his bonds. He picked up a pair of dirty pants from the floor and wandered over to the kid. 'Don't cry, kid, I'm having a great time, it's all part of your education.'

As he pulled his trousers on he turned to Gerda. 'I like kids you know, I wouldn't mind one myself.'

When he had gone back to the shop, Gerda ate the last remaining tomato. There was nothing to eat for the kid, so Gerda took the dummy she secretly kept in her pocket and scraped up all that was left in the ancient rusting tin of Golden Syrup.

The kid sucked the sweetness and quietened down, but her tear-wet eyes still stared in horror.

Gerda looked up through the rotting windows and watched large droplets of rain splash onto the roofscape. Crumbling chimney pots sprouted trees. Guttering hung with weeds and slime.

Christ, what a country, thought Gerda as she curled up on the sofa and fell asleep.

It was dark and raining heavily when she woke.

The kid, still imprisoned by the reins, leaned backwards against the sofa. Her breath was laboured and she was softly sobbing.

Outside, the big man still stood in the flashing lights of the doorway as if he had not moved at all. The sleeping tramp had gone, and the rain had cleaned the space. Regent Street was a blur of lights and wetness in the pounding rain.

⚘

Tony had gone. There was a little wine left in the bottle, Pamela emptied it into her glass. She leaned forward, glass cupped in her hands, brushing her lips against the rim and gazing dreamily across the restaurant, inspecting the other diners.

They all seemed to be enjoying their lunch. On the whole, Pamela decided, they were rather suburban. Not really exciting enough. She would have preferred to see more designer outfits. Daring, stylish, outrageous outfits worn by outrageous and stylish women.

How many little intrigues were going on here? she wondered. How many were wives, how many secretaries, tennis club partners? But no famous faces, not even a minor television star out for a bowl of pasta or a lemon sole.

That was what she wanted, she decided, to be somewhere watching the rich and famous circulate, to see plots of international importance being hatched. To see men taking decisions over their lamb chops that would affect the lives of everyone.

Yes, she decided, she must go more upmarket. She must go where the plants were real. Perhaps she should join a yacht club or take up golf. She carried on musing happily.

People finished their meal and left, others were shown to fresh tables. There was a pleasant movement about the place. She became slowly aware of someone standing very still, not moving at all, on the other side of her table. One piece of flowery fabric put itself between Pamela and the rest of the room.

She looked up and saw Maureen Bell.

Their eyes met and there was a long pause.

'Gotcha,' said Maureen. 'I always thought it was you.'

'I. I. I er . . . It was . . . What are you doing here?'

'Same as you,' said Maureen.

'I er . . . er . . .' Pamela's voice trailed away.

Maureen was triumphant. 'Take it off,' she said, and she sat down firmly on the chair facing her victim. She leaned forward, her nostrils dilated, her eyes burning with hate, voice growling with menace. 'Take it off,' she repeated.

'Oh Maureen, I can't. I'm not wearing a bra.'

'Good,' said Maureen. 'It gets better and better. It's got my name in Indian ink inside the left cuff, hasn't it?'

'Yes, Maureen.'

'Then, my little chum, it's proof positive. You remove it now. This instant. Or it's the police.'

'Oh no, no Maureen. The disgrace.'

Maureen was elated. Her voice grew deeper and deeper with emotion. 'I'll count to five,' she said, and started. 'One . . .'

'I thought you'd be in the office.'

'Dentist,' said Maureen. 'Two . . .'

'There are so many people, Maureen. It's packed.'

'Three . . .'

Pamela had just started on the top button when the waiter brought her a strawberry sorbet. 'Enjoy,' he said.

'Four,' said Maureen in a tone that could not be disobeyed. As she said 'five', the shirt came off. There was a sudden deathly silence in the restaurant which seemed to last for ever.

In slow motion Pamela saw herself surrounded by a sea of faces with various expressions of surprise and delight. From this background Luigi leaped towards her. 'Oh madame,' he cried, and quickly slipped her into her jacket. 'Madame,' he whispered as he covered her up with paper napkins. He actually managed to squeeze her nipples in that brief moment, with all the diners looking on.

Her humiliation was complete, tears flooded her eyes. 'I'm choked, I must go.'

'Stay where you are, you're going to eat.'

'I've eaten, Maureen. I've had a grilled salmon steak.'

'That's nothing to what you're going to eat, my pet.'

Maureen leaned over the table, her face dark and trembling with vengeance.

Pamela looked back at her in bewilderment and disbelief. Only a moment ago it was Tony's kind and loving features facing her over the table, now they were replaced by this terrifying vengeful sight. How the wind could change in just a second. If only she could go back even ten minutes, she might have left the place with Tony.

But she hadn't. She was here, and Maureen was summoning the waiter. 'Bring me a gin,' she said. 'Make it a double.'

'I didn't know you drank,' said Pamela.

'I'm starting now,' said Maureen.

'I never knew you were bossy.'

'How do you think I became an inspector of taxes?'

'You were so quiet at school,' said Pamela.

'Quiet? I was a mouse, a squashed mouse. A quiet little animal tormented by you. I was plain to the point of being repellent. I was picked on by all. But you were my chief persecutor.'

The diners gave quick little glances in their direction, trying desperately to appear as if they weren't really looking.

Maureen swallowed her gin and relaxed her intensity, then lifted her head, letting her shoulders drop.

'Maureen, Maureen,' stammered Pamela. 'I'm sorry I stole your blouse.'

'I'm delighted,' said Maureen, and she summoned the waiter again.

'I will have a Perrier and a small mushroom omelette. Madame will have—'

'Maureen, I told you, I've eaten. I've had a grilled salmon steak on spinach and I've still got this straw-berry sorbet, which I can't face now.' Tears cracked her voice.

'Madame will have,' said Maureen, not lifting her face from the menu, 'duck in orange sauce with the veget-ables of the day. Followed by seafood pasta in cream sauce, and I hope you have a good sweet trolley. Oh, and a bottle of good red wine, I leave the choice to you. That's for madame here, so one glass only please, and in the meantime please bring her a sherry.'

'Maureen, please, please. I can't take red wine, I'm a bit tipsy already,' implored Pamela.

'You'll grow to love red wine,' replied her tormentor. 'You'll be having a lot of it in future, now stop moaning, or you won't be able to eat.'

The sherry tasted strong and burning. It was followed closely by the red wine and the two flavours met in an explosion of unpleasantness in her mouth.

'I feel sick,' said Pamela.

'Not yet,' said Maureen. 'It's much too soon, that joy is yet to come.'

'Enjoy,' said the waiter as he put the duck before her.

The sauce on the duck was a very dark brown with little globules of fat floating on the surface. A few pieces of tinned mandarins lay half-submerged on the side. It was accompanied by overcooked cauliflower and a good helping of potatoes.

Pamela picked up her knife and fork and took a small mouthful. It tasted strongly of gravy powder and grease. She lifted her eyes beseechingly, only to meet Maureen's dazzling smile.

'Clean up your plate like a good girl,' she said. 'I can see this is going to be fun. Maybe one of these days you'll throw up in a restaurant. At peak time, with a bit of luck,' and she refilled Pamela's glass.

Under Maureen's fearsome gaze, Pamela painfully swallowed the awful stuff.

'Wipe your plate with the bread.'

'Maureen, no, no, Maureen.'

'Do it.'

Tears were softly slipping down Pamela's face when the waiter put the seafood pasta on the table. 'Enjoy,' he said again.

She looked up in despair. 'I can't,' she said. 'I must go.'

'Stay where you are,' snapped Maureen. 'Eat it, bloody well eat it. And get on with the wine, you've still got half a bottle.'

Miserably, with downcast eyes, Pamela forced the food down her throat. She lifted her eyes again only to meet her torturer's dazzling smile.

'Eat, Pamela, eat.'

'Have pity on me, Maureen.'

Maureen lifted the slice of lemon from her glass of water, sucked the juice, then put the rind in the middle of the seafood pasta. 'And how many times, little friend, little pet, did you have pity on me? I was eighteen when I walked out of that school, we started primary school on the same day, aged five. You picked me out on day one. Day *one*. And you hit the target until that final parents' day. Let me put more cream on your meringue.' She smiled.

Jottings

Pamela could hardly see the meringue, it was just a vague white shape. She made helpless little jabs at it with her spoon. Everything beyond the orbit of her table was just a blur, an occasional spot of colour from a bright dress. 'Can't, can't,' whispered Pamela.

Maureen beamed across the table. 'My little pal,' she said. 'Indulge yourself. I'll see you home. We'll have lots more little jaunts like this. Lots and lots of them.'

The coffee came with the chocolate mints and liqueur. Maureen's face seemed to be just a pair of eyes floating in a mist. Pamela could no longer feel her limbs, voices came as though through a long tunnel. She was scarcely aware that after the nightmare of the gargantuan meal, Maureen took one elbow, Luigi the other, and escorted her to the door.

Maureen wrapped the offending shirt round her neck and acknowledged the sympathetic glances of the other diners with the air of a martyr. The group of waiters at the door giggled openly.

'She's trying to overcome it.' Maureen spoke to an elderly couple as she passed their table.

'Oh, we know all about it,' they said in a conspiratorial whisper, turkey jowls wobbling. 'We've got it in the family. They need a lot of help and understanding. It's a good job she's got you.'

The laughing waiters waved them off in the taxi.

❀

It seemed to Pamela that she had been hours in the downstairs cloakroom, throwing up. Eventually, she managed to crawl upstairs on her hands and knees, then got into Daddy's dressing gown before she passed out.

It was dark when she woke and she felt she wanted to die. She couldn't bear the idea of lights. Clinging to the balustrade she slid her bare feet down each step until she came to the hall. In the gloom she reached the back of the stairs when Gerda came in, shut the door with her back and leaned against it with the child in her arms.

'I think de kid, she hev asthma again,' she said.

The child stared through the dark at Pamela. Each in their altered state, they gazed at each other. The kid was as neat and tidy as she had been that morning. She wore exactly the same clothes, but her breathing was laboured and there was a little sob in her throat.

Pamela stared silently at her for a very long time. She said, 'That's not my kid.'

❀

Now Pamela was alone with the kid.

The leaves were drifting off the trees. Everything looked grey. The sky. The houses. Grey people in grey streets. Here she was. In the house. All alone, except for the child. Gerda had left with an American family who had places in Miami and New York. Pamela's mother had developed a sudden interest in literature and was away on seemingly endless holidays of writers' circles. Bernard she could only reach by fax, and every time she made an appeal to him, he sent money.

By now she had a lot of money. She could buy endless beautiful holidays to glamorous parts of the world. There was nothing to stop her. Except the kid. Her world here had come to a full stop. What was happening to her now was too horrible to contemplate.

She had the means. She had the money to fly, to reappear on the far side of the world, somewhere Maureen had never heard of, to be someone else, to start afresh.

She could go tomorrow, but for the kid. It wasn't even her kid. The more intimately she lived with her, she knew it wasn't her kid. She felt so alone now, and friendless. The greatest blow had been when she had lost Tony.

True to her word, Maureen had taken her to more epic meals. Each one more horrific than the last. The food was richer. There was more of it. The drinks grew stronger, and each meal found her more bloated and drunken than the last. Maureen threatened her with the Savoy, the Ritz and the Dorchester.

Pamela could not settle. She roamed the house in despair, waiting for the dreaded phone call from Maureen that would summon her to hell, and at the same time, beating her breast in anguish that she had lost Tony. 'Oh Tony, Tony,' she cried out loud as she roamed the empty house.

She could only console herself now with a small glass of the drink she had started to keep in the cupboard. Her terrible punishment was creating its own appetite. She couldn't face her days now without a dose of her torture. She lived, over and over again, the moment she had lost Tony.

It was in Luigi's. Maureen had chosen the selfsame spot for a further humiliation, even the same table. It was so close in pattern, it seemed like the same meal.

She was presented with two large sherries on arrival. She had red wine with the prawns in a rich sauce. Again she had the duck in the thick dark sauce and two pathetic pieces of tinned mandarin. More red wine with that.

With lamb curry she had vodka. With zabaglione an added glass of Marsala. Her meringue had extra cream. Her coffee and chocolates were served with cognac and a cherry brandy.

By now she did not protest. No longer did she lift her head and appeal to Maureen; that only added to her humiliation. Pamela kept her head down and grovelled, eating and drinking in utter desperation.

Maureen sat watching her in a glow of contentment, sipping her designer water, always throwing the chewed lemon peel into the middle of Pamela's plate. She never ate more than a small omelette and a piece of watercress herself.

'Madame has good appetite,' said the waiter.

'She enjoys her food,' said Maureen. 'I come with her to let her indulge and then I can see her home.'

'You are good friend, madame.' The waiter looked emotional and had to turn his head away.

'We went to school together,' said Maureen. 'We go back a long way.'

Luigi kept his eye on them and when the moment came, Maureen turned and beckoned him. Silently they each took an arm, holding it round their necks. Pamela's head hung lolling, like a newly slaughtered animal. She trailed her feet between their tread, she dribbled heavily from her open mouth.

A hush fell on the diners, a few shrieks and giggles from women who were half drunk themselves, as they watched her progress to the door. Some people were leaving and nipped extra-quickly through the door. A small group was just entering the restaurant.

Leading the group was Tony. On his arm, a very distinguished elderly lady. Behind her, two men whose gimlet eyes swept the room. Her bodyguards.

Pamela flickered her eyes towards her long enough to recognize her from photographs in newspapers. But her eyes focused on Tony's horrified expression. His face was a picture of unbelief. His mouth twisted with disgust. He visibly shuddered, at the same time turning to his precious companion, putting a protective arm to shield her from the horrible sight.

Pamela never heard from him again. His secretary always said he was out at a meeting. If he answered the phone himself, he simply put it down with 'Excuse me'. Her letters, torn up like confetti, were returned in mauve envelopes.

Once she went to his showroom but was asked to leave by his assistant. She waited outside but he swept past and into a taxi as if she were invisible. She got the message. It was over. She had lost her only friend.

❀

She hadn't bothered to dress. What was the use? She wrapped herself in Daddy's dressing gown. She could smell his tobacco on the rough wool. She could also smell the vomit from the last two visits to restaurants with Maureen.

She roamed restlessly. She took another bottle of whisky out of the cupboard. It was empty.

'Damn you,' she screamed to the empty kitchen. 'Damn you,' she screamed into the grinning face of the statue of Pan.

The leer on his white china face seemed to be saying something to her. The gold of his horns gleamed against the potted palms.

'You complacent shit,' she screamed at him. 'You just keep looking at me with your eyes, your grinning eyes.' And she lifted the bottle high, bringing it crashing down, shattering his china head all over the floor.

With trembling hands, she took a fresh bottle of whisky. Glass in one hand, bottle in the other, once again she roamed the house.

Waiting.

Waiting for the telephone to ring. Waiting for the summons. Why, why must she be doing this, when she herself could pick up the phone and book a flight to China or Bali?

She finally flopped into the sofa. There was no sound in the grey day except for a stray piece of ivy lashing on the windows like a whip. She stared in the gloom at the phone which was just by her eyeline.

At any moment it would ring with another hideous invitation she must obey.

From the playpen in the corner, the kid watched her mother with sad, dark eyes, her face pressed against the bars.

Pamela gazed back. With frozen lips, she whispered, 'That's not my kid'.

The Stockings

Dragonby, 1934

She knew the old woman was dead when she smelled the burning bedding in the garden.

She had gone to throw an empty tin into the dustbin, but now, with it still in her hand, she stood in the deep, damp cold; such cold as is only found in low-lying flat country in the early days of the year.

Fog hung thick and still, hiding even the gnarled old apple tree in the garden. It pressed the smell of the burning bedding downwards, holding it as if in an upturned cup over the two ugly cottages in the long muddy lane.

There were no other dwellings in sight. A straggly hedge grew on either side of the land and beyond that lay flat muddy fields where sugar beet, potatoes and turnips grew, in their turn.

Phyllis felt a shudder run down her spine as she stood

there, then she turned abruptly and threw the tin into the bin.

By comparison with the world outside even her kitchen looked cosy to her when she returned. She raised the wick of the oil lamp a little higher, restlessly stirred the fire, and then tried to get a little music from the radio. This came through quite gaily for a few minutes then rapidly faded into a faraway dim sound.

'Damn the accumulator,' said Phyllis as she switched it off.

She felt strangely agitated as her eyes searched the familiar room, the old black stove that was her daily toil, the ugly furniture, brown paint everywhere, the large rag rug made by her late mother-in-law, and the oil lamp. She hated this kitchen, which had neither electricity nor convenience. And beyond the kitchen was the damp, dark scullery with a single cold tap, where little pools of water collected on the worn tiled floor.

Only a candle was allowed out there; Fred was firm about that. She must not waste oil, must watch every penny. It had been good enough for his parents. It would do for him. He dismissed his wife's desire for greater comfort with a shrug of his shoulders. She would get used to it in time.

Resentment burned suddenly within her. She banged her fist hard against the shabby radio. Pushing herself between the table and chairs, she brought her fist down again and again on the sideboard, on the table, on each chair, until she felt suddenly weak and tears sprang to her eyes. Then she sat down and stared into the fire.

So the old woman was gone from the house next door. Phyllis had been expecting it, for the district nurse had told her, as she wheeled her bicycle down the lane, how bad the seizure was.

The surly couple, her son and daughter-in-law, would be glad to have the old woman gone from their hearth. She had been a great burden to them and they made no secret of the fact. But Phyllis knew she would miss the old woman; since her marriage she had known no other friend.

She looked at the shabby wooden armchair as it stood beside her in the firelight and pictured the old woman as she sat there hour after hour. They had gossiped, drunk endless cups of strong tea and relived their lives over and over again. Phyllis had not much to tell for she was yet young, but the old woman was long past seventy and she had much to relate.

No detail was forgotten as she sat in the chair, her thin, colourless hair screwed back from her face. She was toothless, and as she talked the saliva gathered at the corners of her mouth, then trickled down until it met a large wart, out of which grew strong black hairs. As Phyllis gazed into her face she never failed to be fascinated by this and tried to guess to which side of the wart the stream of saliva would roll.

The old woman's hands were stained with deeply ingrained dirt. She always wore a vast black skirt, shiny with grease, and a brown crocheted shawl over a dark blouse. This outfit remained constant through hot summer and icy winter. Even the white woollen stockings were worn throughout the year.

Phyllis never ceased to wonder how the stockings were ever washed, for they were worn every day. Perhaps they were washed at night sometimes and dried quickly in front of the fire. Perhaps that was why they turned a dirty yellow colour, stained with food and sweat. Phyllis had known it was always the same pair of stockings because of a rip at one ankle, a fair-sized hole with blackened edges. It had been burned one day as they sat by the fire. The old woman, so carried away by her story, had failed to notice the cinder that had fallen out of the fire, and by the time she jumped up with the sharp little pain, her stocking had a smouldering hole at the side.

'I'll mend that sometime,' she would say. But the hole had still been there on her last visit, only days ago.

The dead woman had worn gold earrings threaded through wrinkled holes in her unclean ears. They were the pride of her life, her earrings, for Joe had bought them whilst they were on their honeymoon. The honeymoon had lasted four days. They wouldn't have had one but Joe had an aunt living at Edmonton, so they only had the fares to pay.

On their second day there, in the evening, they'd had several drinks and sung lustily by the piano in the public house. Coming out into the cool night they had walked along, arms entwined, his hat on the back of his head, hers a saucy upturned basket of roses. They sang as they walked. Seeing a pawnshop sifting its yellow beams of light through the unredeemed jewellery, they had stopped and fallen silent.

'You should have earrings with that hat,' said Joe, and in a golden daze they bought the golden hearts to hang in her ears. 'Your heart and mine,' said Joe.

That was the first romantic thing he had said, and it was the last. They had never again recaptured the glow of that evening. Life, hard and relentless, had begun in earnest the next day when they returned to the little farm labourer's cottage.

Now the old woman was dead, and the child conceived on that radiant evening long ago was a surly ugly man who was relieved to see his mother go.

With a sigh, Phyllis rose and began to shred cheese and onion into a tin. This she placed in the oven to await

Fred. He would eat it, she knew, with thick chunks of bread, silently, thoroughly, occasionally drinking deeply from the pint mug of strong black tea beside him on the table. He was late tonight, but Phyllis could not guess at the time he would return as a cow was in calf and he would stay with her until it was born.

She opened the back door and looked out into the night. She could see only a solid wall of fog that advanced upon her in long drifts as she stood there. She shuddered and closed the door.

Picking up a newspaper she tried to read but the silence seemed to envelop her; a silence wrapped in deep, icy cold fog. She stood for one moment not knowing what to do, then, feeling she must make a clatter, do something active, she drew some hot water from the brass tap by the fire and proceeded to wash Fred's overalls. They were very dirty.

She rubbed them hard between her clenched hands and the work seemed to bring her satisfaction as she made a great din with the bucket and bowl. Silly to hang them on the line, she thought, they would not dry at all, but at least they would sweeten in the process.

She picked up the bucket and walked carefully round the side of the house. Lifting her head in the darkness, she found the line, then picking up a pair of the overalls she hung them on the line. With two pegs in her mouth,

Dragonby. 1934

LIZ SMITH

she lifted a second pair, heavy with water, and then slid her fingers along the frozen line.

They touched something unexpected. Her chilled fingers opened, letting the overalls fall to the ground. Phyllis placed her hand on the two strange objects, pulled them from the line, and carried them into the veiled glow of light coming from the kitchen window.

But she knew what they were before she even saw them. They were the old woman's stockings.

Her suddenly beating heart was the only sound to be heard in the all-consuming silence. Then she started in anger. Those people next door, they were beasts to play a trick like that! It must be to show their displeasure at her friendship with their mother, of which she knew they did not approve although they had never spoken to her. Now they had done this thing, and the woman so lately dead.

With an abrupt movement, she threw the stockings into the dustbin, hung up the overalls and went into the house. She sat in front of the fire and warmed herself. Tomorrow she would take the radio accumulator into Thornton and collect the other one. At least she could then have a bit of music, hear people's voices to break the silence.

Her weekly shopping trip was the one bright spot in her life. She would look at all the latest ladies' wear that

62

the shops of Thornton had to offer, perhaps buy a bag of sweets to eat in the bus on the way home. Sometimes she would meet someone she knew. They would enquire about every member of each other's family, then, falling silent, would bid each other farewell. There was no more contact. She had nothing to offer. Her marriage to Fred, a farmhand, had not enlarged her horizon.

Phyllis was a Thornton girl, an orphan brought up by her aunt. She had worked in the large cut-price sweet shop opposite the bus station. There she had giggled with several girls of her own age, through the jars of coloured sweets, remarking on the passengers as they exited the buses.

It was most exciting on a Saturday, when so many people made their weekly trip into the busy little provincial town, where prominent among the visitors were the young lads from the farms. With faces newly scrubbed, they stood in groups on the street corners and made loud remarks to each other. They would laugh heartily and long, and then would stroll around the market, buying bags of fruit and sweets. It was always a flag day on Saturday, so they would each buy one and wear it in their caps, carefully placing it with big, red hands by the button at the side. Then they would go to the pictures or the dance hall.

Fred had never quite belonged to any particular group.

He had always stood alone and solemnly watched the traffic go by. This excited Phyllis' interest in him from the start. He was so much bigger than the others were, too. She sighed as she peered through the glass bottles.

The other girls, Vi and Madge, laughed and flirted with the country boys but picked two who lived in the town to be their husbands. Phyllis had tried to keep up her friendships with these girls, but years passed and they had moved far away, and letters between them had become more and more infrequent until they had finally stopped.

The aunt who had brought her up had died. Her uncle and his new wife made it obvious she was not welcome in their home. One by one doors closed against her. She was shut out from the rest of the world, alone with the large silent man, the dark little cottage, and with only the old woman to talk to.

Her trip to Thornton the following day was not a success. The fog lifted only slightly in the middle of the day and had thickened again by mid-afternoon. A sense of desolation seemed to oppress her. The lane seemed longer than ever, her shopping heavier.

Fred came home with wet feet. There were no clean socks in his drawer.

'Maybe there's a pair in this lot,' she said, and thrust her hand into the pile of clothing airing on the hob. One by one she felt the articles with her fingers, searching for the touch of wool, but when she touched wool, it was not the texture of Fred's socks, but over-washed knitting, thick and felted. Her fingers found a hole. She drew the old woman's stockings from the pile.

'What are those damned things?' said Fred. 'Chuck them away and find me my socks. Come on, I'm hungry, I want my supper.'

For one moment she gazed at the stockings and a sudden terror held her heart. Why were they there, how could they be when she had thrown them away herself? With a fearful glance round, as if expecting to see the old woman standing in the shadows, Phyllis turned and thrust them in the fire. She held them there with a poker, watched them blacken and turn to a cinder. She dropped a heavy piece of coal onto the fire and watched the fragile cinder break up.

A day passed and another came: the day of the funeral. Phyllis watched between the drawn curtains of the musty front parlour.

It was such a sad little funeral, three mourners, the son, his wife and their son, sitting solidly in the hired car. The hearse lurched and squelched down the muddy lane. Her last view was of the entourage disappearing at a speed that was just a little too fast, in order, it would seem, to have the whole thing over and done with.

That night Phyllis could not sleep. The next morning she was heavy-eyed and dull in spirit. The fog did not lift at all during that day.

Restlessly she turned from one task to another. She polished the worn lino, and then turned out the kitchen cupboard. In case it had been dirtied in the process, she polished the floor again, the brown-painted furniture too, then looked around for another job, although it was nearly evening.

She remembered there were some blankets needing darning and went upstairs in the icy darkness. Knowing where to find the old chest of drawers without a light, she knelt down and reached out for the blankets – but her hands picked up the old woman's stockings. Had she not destroyed them in the fire? She knelt there holding them. A feeling of despair pressed down upon her and her loneliness was intense.

She would be rid of the stockings. She would. She knew of a place.

Out through the front door she went, the stockings held in her folded arms pressed against her breast.

Phyllis slithered down the lane and stumbled in the mud, not in the direction that led to the road, but the opposite way. The darkness was disturbed only by the white arms of fog that drifted over the scrawny hedge and her breath as it whitened before her.

She knew where the stockings would be safe. The green pond was said to be bottomless in the middle. She must take them there herself and bury them deep down in the slime, right in the middle of the pond. She could not swim but no matter, she would walk on the bottom of the pond until she reached the bottomless bit and she would push the stockings far down.

The old woman wouldn't find them there. Phyllis would hide them. She would find a way. She laughed softly to herself, then louder, and louder. She was still laughing when she started to wade into the pond.

Her last laugh left a few little bubbles on the water, but they soon disappeared.

The Shopkeeper stood waiting

Beatles

I was too early for the film so I went over the road to the hardware shop. It was a cavernous place, entirely covered with merchandise, every inch lined with objects for sale, suitable for every section of the house.

In the halfway distance stood the shopkeepers, anxious and waiting. I felt frozen with fear of not finding something I wanted. With their eyes upon me, I searched.

In the background, the radio played the Beatles singing 'All You Need is Love'. I finally paid 59p for a plastic tea strainer. They put it in a bag.

The beat went on. 'All you need is love.' Something I had never realized before was how very slowly the Beatles sang.

How very very slow.

'All you need is love.'

Eliza's Story

Chapter 1

In October 1908, the weather suddenly turned very cold.

A chill wind whistled down the narrow cobbled streets of Clecklewyke and grabbed the rough woollen skirts of Eliza Northrop as she hurried towards Sarah Street.

It had been a hard day. Tuesday. A day she hated. The day she did the weekly wash for Mrs Tinsley.

Mrs Tinsley always had a lot of washing. She had three daughters who seemed to change their underwear more than was necessary.

The wash house, at the back of the kitchen, did not drain properly, and the water splashed from the tubs and stood in icy cold pools, soaking the cardboard-thin soles of Eliza Northrop's boots. She had put a fold of newspaper over the hole in the toe, and now it was turning to a slippery mess as she made her way over the uneven pavements.

The streets were steep and hard to climb when you were tired. When you were carrying heavy bags, or carrying a baby, inside or outside the womb.

The tiny terraced houses were packed together, rising tier upon tier, connected by little alleyways. Built of red brick, they had stood so long under the pall of soot-filled smoke from the factories that they had developed a thin crust of shale which shone blue from a distance.

There had been no plan to separate the workers from the works. It was merely a blunt statement. Here were the works, and there were the workers. So the huge, aggressive industries were set down with a firm and uncompromising hand.

Brass foundries. Iron. Steel foundries. Tap and washer works.

Heavy engineering, manufacturing gargantuan parts for ships being made in Scotland to sail to the furthest parts of the Empire.

They were dirty works. Enormous, black monsters belching out jets of steam, fire and smoke, while beating the ear with terrible noise, screams of whistles, clanging of machinery, thumping of steam-driven pistons. In the wool factories the people had to lip-read because of the hideous clamour.

Down at the back sides of the works lay the passive canals quietly receiving the filthy chemical-filled slime that oozed from the industry. In the canals immediately outside the works, fish floated stiff and white, upside down in the murky water, their pearlized eyes gazing fixedly at the gloomy sky. Further upstream, men fished on Sundays.

Tall, blackened walls surrounded these horrors of the industrial revolution. Walls that vibrated with the pent-up energy within, as if, at any moment, they too might burst open and flood the pavement with molten metal or streams of scalding steam.

The houses started immediately outside the walls, then rose, street by cobbled street, to the blue-black church which stood at the highest point.

It was a huge church, grim and foreboding, like an angry parent ever frowning down on its helpless children. Holding them in fear, threatening them with death and damnation because they were such sinners.

I'd like the chance to sin a bit, thought Eliza often as she passed the dark edifice. Sometimes she wished she were Catholic, at least they had candles and warm-smelling incense. Mostly she was too weary to go to church. But occasionally the vicar would come hammering on her door and say he had not seen her repenting her sins lately. Then she would make an effort and creep to the back of the congregation, hoping the vicar would notice she was there.

But he always seemed so far away, shouting up there in the pulpit, and there were some well-dressed folk between her and the altar. They stood so pious and superior that the only sensation she seemed to have was one of envy at the cut of a cloth coat, its fur trimming, or the swathe of velvet on a Sunday hat.

In fact, when she was in church, Eliza hardly thought about God at all. But that did not bother her because she realized He would be much more interested in the well-off folk in there. That must be so because the vicar cared so much more for them.

Eliza did not resent the lack of interest in herself, it left her free to drift and dream, not listening to the sermon, but watching the congregation. When the plate was passed, her penny looked so small that she placed it down with her hand flat over it so the church warden could not see.

Bill, Eliza's husband, never went to church. He did not see the need to pretend, ever. He was what he was and that was it. He enjoyed being a drunken lout. It suited him and he had no ambition to be anything else.

He had a roof over his head, leaky though it was. He had his cronies at the Hare and Hounds. He very rarely went hungry, usually there would be enough to eat. Liza would see to that.

When times were bad, and they often were, for Bill could not hold on to work very long, Eliza would take on yet another cleaning job, bring home a little more money and leftovers from the plates of the better-off wrapped up in old newspaper.

Bill thought of it as his right, for he considered himself a handsome man and if there was any reluctance on Eliza's part to slave for him, a few sharp blows around the head and shoulders soon brought her to her senses.

Eliza would have been happy to go to chapel. She would have preferred it with its simple service and straightforward talking. Often she had passed the door of the chapel when they were having an evening of singing and poetry.

The little girls wore white dresses with satin sashes at these affairs, and Eliza wished she were in there with them. But she dare not put her foot over the doorway, for most of her employers were chapel people and it would not do if she were to meet them face to face in God's house.

Imagine the look on the face of Alderman Helliwell, if he was standing there, saying 'Good morning', handing out hymn books, and in walked Eliza Northrop. Eliza Northrop, who did all his family's washing in the dark, dank, wash house. Eliza Northrop, who scrubbed all the tiled floors twice a week along with the front steps. Mrs Northrop who, once a week, took the pile of saved-up tea leaves then sprinkled them all over the carpets in every room, including the spare bedroom, right down the stairs over the richly patterned Turkish carpet, and the rug in front of the hallstand as far as the front door.

Having put tea leaves on every inch of carpet in the house, she then took a dustpan and brush and swept them off, the damp leaves collecting the dust as they went into the pan.

It was an awkward job in heavy skirts, which Eliza had to hook around her. Ruby Birtle, who worked as a maid for Alderman Helliwell and his wife, often laughed, because she said that when she did the carpets, Eliza showed her drawers. It was difficult to do the carpets and steps without showing a bit of leg. Maybe Alderman Helliwell had caught sight of a bit above the ankle when she had been down there scrubbing his floors.

So how could she walk through that door one Sunday morning and expect him to say 'Good morning', and hand her a prayer book?

Besides, she had head lice. She had grown used to living with their movement, but if she went to a service and stood in a row with the others, maybe one would drop down onto her shoulders, even run along the back of a chair onto the shoulders of a respectable person, someone in a decent coat, maybe black-faced cloth with a beaver collar, perhaps a hat with osprey feather trim.

Eliza shuddered at the thought and never went to the

chapel in case it should ever happen like that. As for going to the Hare and Hounds, well, that didn't matter, they all had lice there.

No. She was better to make her occasional trips to the Church of England. Sit right at the back ready to jump thankfully through the door, into the air.

She knew where she was in the Church of England; they let her know her place in life. Which was right at the bottom of the pile.

Another gust of cold wind hit her as she crossed Mafeking Street, and a few drops of rain touched her face. Her big toe suddenly burst through the hole in her coarse cotton stocking and she bent down to try and make her feet more comfortable.

As she fiddled with her boot laces she remembered it was her birthday. Forty-nine today. She was an ageing woman. The pattern of her life was running unchanging and was now leading only to old age.

No one would remember her birthday. A shudder ran through her body and she stood carefully adjusting her weight for the rheumatism in her knees.

No. Damn it, she wouldn't go straight home, she'd treat herself to a bit of cake at Martha Woodthorpe's.

As Eliza entered the little parlour through the front door, Martha walked in from the back room and smiled warmly at her. 'Hello Liza, love. It's grand to see you.'

ELIZA.
1908

'I'm glad you're not closed yet, Martha,' said Eliza. 'I see you've got some Bakewell tart left.'

'Yes, I have. Would you like some?'

'Oh yes,' said Eliza. 'You make the best Bakewell tart of anybody I know.'

Eliza felt suddenly relaxed and the tart was delicious.

'Where have you been today, Liza?'

'Tinsleys' today, Wellington Road. Three lasses, mister and missus, old Grandma, doesn't leave her bed.'

'Does she wet it?

'All the time.'

They laughed together.

'There's going to be a big do there soon,' Eliza announced.

'What sort of a do?'

'Silver wedding; and not just them. There was three couples married on the same day you see. There was Albert and Annie Parker, Herbert and Clara Soppitt, and the Helliwells. They was all wed together, at the same ceremony, by the same person, in Lane End chapel.'

'That's a funny idea, their getting married at once.'

'They were right friendly, you see. And they still are. Well, in a way. Everybody's got to come out on top, all stabbing each other in the back. That's why this do has to be better than anybody else's.'

'Is Mrs H having a new frock?' said Martha.

'Oh blooming heck, is she? That there poor bloody dressmaker has been up to that bloody house so many times, she doesn't know whether she's coming or going. They're mean buggers. But they've always got to show off. Always got to do everything better than the next one.'

❀

The rain was falling heavily by the time she reached Sarah Street. Her front door key hung on a piece of string just inside the letter box, she pulled it through and let herself into the tiny dark parlour.

The ancient wallpaper of a depressing violet colour was peeling away from the walls, which were now running with the rain beating through the broken roof. There was a thin stream of rain, too, over the stairs and one in the bedroom.

Automatically, Eliza collected an old pail, a chamber pot and a basin, putting them under each leak. It was standard procedure whenever the rain came, for the roof was never mended.

There was a black horse-hair sofa against one wall and a wooden high-backed chair by the fireplace. The fireplace was of iron, a mean design with the basket high up on the wall, the whole thing was painted dark green and above the narrow mantelpiece was an overmantel where cheap little china ornaments stood, mainly mementoes of fairs, or a day in Blackpool.

The small table in the middle of the room was covered with a torn chenille cloth, thrown out by one of Eliza's employers. In the centre of the cloth was a glass tureen containing a stuffed bird sitting on a heap of wax fruit. The glass was cracked and the sad display was covered with dust.

There were three pictures on the mouldy walls. The enlarged sepia portrait of Bill's grandmother stared out of her frame with a look of determined grimness in her gimlet eyes. A double portrait of Bill's mother and father, each face wearing a look of utter dismay at finding themselves in this world. Then there was the very shadowy picture of George, as a baby.

George was taken by his mother to the photographers at the early age of six months, in case, like all the other babies she'd had, he too might die.

But the frames of the portraits had not long to survive, for the damp was taking them apart. Already the backs of the pictures were thick with green mould and blackened specks were covering the faces.

By now, Eliza wanted to pee. She opened the back door and looked into the yard. The battered wooden doors ended about eight inches above the floor and she could see the feet of someone sitting in each closet.

So she had no choice but to use the chamber pot and put it back to catch the raindrops.

The back room was completely dominated by the big rough table, there were a few chairs round it, and everything happened on it. It held dirty iron saucepans, several cracked mugs, Bill's iron foot and hammers for mending his boots, his shaving brush and mug, a cracked piece of mirror for his ablutions, a pile of dirty clothes and a whole heap of plants and grasses that George had picked from the canal bank.

Eliza sighed and started to clean the saucepans. She fetched some water from the tap in the yard and emptied it into a container built into the fireplace. She had to light the fire to heat the water, so she cleaned out the cinders in the grate and took the coal bucket down to the cellar.

The way to the cellar was through the cupboard with their only shelves for food storage, which caused everything to smell and taste of coal dust.

The coal was damp and slow to light, but eventually the water became warm enough to tackle the saucepans. They were not easy. The beef stew was cooked well into the worn surface of the iron pots.

Eliza dipped her fingers into the scouring powder and pressed round and round the pots with her hand until at least some of the mess had come off. Then she felt hungry.

There was a tripe shop in a front room only three doors away, so she went and bought a pound of tripe and two boiled pig's feet. When she got back Bill was sitting at the table, trimming his moustache in the cracked piece of mirror. He was a vain man.

'What have you got to eat?' he said, still with his eyes on his moustache. 'Owt or nowt?'

'It's never nowt, is it, you daft beggar?' she replied. 'I always find summat, don't I?'

'I hope it's not pig's feet again,'said Bill.

'Well it is then, and there's a bit of tripe.'

I fancied chitterlings,' said Bill, 'or a bit of black pudding,' and he twisted his mouth in the broken glass to get a sharp shape to his moustache.

'How did you do today?' said Eliza. 'Get owt?'

'Nowt!' he replied.

'You won't be coming to the pub tonight then?'

'I am that. I've got a return game with Jack Parker. And you can buy me a few pints.'

'I'm sick of buying you a few pints, it's time you bought your own.'

'Shut up, woman, or you'll feel the back of my hand.'

Eliza grimaced as she sorted out the tripe, for she knew he meant it.

Later on, she sat with the women in the Hare and Hounds and watched Bill playing dominoes. He swept his fingers over the dominoes as if he were playing a great concerto. He constantly touched his moustache until the ends turned up sharply, and, as he did so, he turned and smiled at Ada.

Ada was sitting with the women, only three seats away from Eliza, but Bill leered at her shamelessly. Ada turned and grinned triumphantly at Eliza. Ada, with her ragged feather boa, a bunch of violets in her battered little hat and an eye-catching pair of earrings, had every reason to feel triumphant, for not only had she attracted Bill, but she was able to flirt with him in front of his wife for added excitement.

The other women grunted sympathetically through the froth on their stout, at the same time observing, 'She's younger than you an' all, Liza.' Life was raw and they spoke frankly.

'Aye, you're right,' concurred Eliza. 'She's no more than thirty-five, and tonight I'm forty-nine.'

'Forty-nine?' they chorused. 'Is it your birthday, love?'

'It is that,' said Eliza and finished her pot of beer.

'Then you shall have a gin,' they all agreed.

Unable to buy one out of a single pocket, the women clubbed together and bought her a large gin. It slipped down her throat to join the several pots of beer and Eliza felt warm and relaxed. Nothing mattered any more – the work that awaited her tomorrow; Bill and Ada; Bill with his big beefy arms hitting her round her head and body. Everything went into a pleasant haze, and she joined in the singing with a loud, lusty voice.

'Thanks lasses,' she said. 'I suppose I'd better be getting myself back to Sarah Street,' and she rose on unsteady legs.

'Are you going somewhere right nice tomorrow?' enquired her companions.

'Nice? Nice?' Eliza's voice was slurred. 'I'm bloody not. Back to those flaming Helliwells. More cleaning. Cleaning every corner of that damned house for that do they're having.'

Out in the street, before she set out for home, she had an overwhelming desire to pass water, so she felt her way round the wall and into the alley at the side of the pub doorway. She squatted down to relieve herself but found it very difficult to rise with the rheumatic pains in her knees.

As she leaned against the wall, her eyes growing used to the darkness, she became aware she was not alone in the alleyway. Two people were there. Two people copulating, pressed hard against the wet wall. The man grunting. The woman gasping.

Even in the blackness she knew it was Bill, and she could see the gleam of Ada's earrings. Her knees throbbed with pain and seemed to set.

Bill finished with a scream and withdrew from Ada. He turned and sensing someone was there he lit a match.

'What the hell are you crouching down there for?' he shouted at Eliza at the same time bringing his open hand heavily across her face. 'Get up, you stupid bitch,' and he struck her again.

He pulled her to her feet and pushed her down the street. Eliza was still drunk and she staggered as he pushed her in front of him. Angry that she had witnessed his copulation, he hit her repeatedly around her head and shoulders all the way home. Blood trickled from Eliza's nose, and, mixing with tears, dripped into her mouth. She tasted the salt on her tongue as she licked it away.

'What's the matter, Mam?' said George when he saw her.

George sat pale and fat, at the kitchen table, lit from above in the pale green glow from the gas mantle. He was sorting out the grasses and plants he had collected by the canal. His concern made his fat jowls droop and he looked like an ivory Buddha.

Bill lurched over the table and swept the grasses onto the floor.

'What are you doing, Dad? I've been right up to Darnley for those. They're rare they are, I've been on my bicycle all day to get them.'

'Rare are they?' shouted Bill. 'I'll make them rarer.

What kind of a silly sod have I got for a son? A damn fool who collects grass,' and he hit out at George.

But for all his bulk, George was quick on his feet and usually managed to evade his father.

'You don't want 'em chucked on the floor? You great nancy, collecting grass! Well,' said Bill, 'we'll take them off the floor.' And with that he picked up the plants and thrust them into the remaining coals of the fire.

'No, Dad! No!' cried George in agony. He made a move towards the smouldering grass but his father stood brandishing a poker in front of the fireplace.

Bill turned towards Eliza with a snarl. 'You raised one whelp out of the litter and look at it. A big, soft, daft idiot what collects grass. Grass and weeds.'

Eliza leaned against the wall, tears coursing down her swollen face. For it was true, out of all the children she had borne, only George had survived. Five times she had sweated and groaned in the grim room upstairs to produce a dead or dying baby. George, fat and ugly though he was, had survived with his quiet acceptance of life.

From the very beginning, he had smiled and reached out whenever he had seen a flower, but in Sarah Street that was very rare. Now he would cycle for miles to search the hedgerows and the canalside. He would go to the free library to find the names of the plants and these he noted in a book with a little drawing of his own.

Bill removed his trousers before he got into bed, keeping on his vest, flannel shirt, long pants and socks. Eliza turned back the dark grey blankets.

'It's cold tonight,' said Bill. 'Put summat else on.'

She added his jacket and her own coat then crept wearily into bed beside him. The rain dripped through the roof and made regular drops into the chamber pot.

Eliza lay flat on her back, her face and arms now throbbing with pain. She looked up at the blackened ceiling and watched the damp patch spread in the faint glow of the gas lamp fluttering outside in the street.

'It was my birthday today,' she whispered. 'I was forty-nine today. Did you hear that, Bill? I was forty-nine today.'

Bill stirred under the damp coats. 'You're old. Ada's only thirty-five.'

The next day, Ruby Birtle made great fun of her bruises. She leaned against the wall laughing.

'So, did you trip up over the step again? You look right funny with them black eyes, not one, but two. I wonder what you did to deserve that.'

Eliza was in no mood to banter. 'Just tell me what she wants me to do today will you, and shut up.'

'Beds today, stripped right down.'

'Not right down?' said Eliza.

'Right down,' confirmed Ruby.

'Down to the last feather?' Not feathers an' all?'

'Aye. But don't worry, lass.' Ruby suddenly felt the need to console Eliza when she saw how exhausted and beaten she looked. 'Daft Madge is up there, she's been at it a couple of days now.'

Eliza made for the stairs.

'She's on the second landing,' called Ruby.

'I can see she is,' said Eliza, as the feathers drifted across her face.

There, on the attic stairs, crouched daft Madge in a sea of feathers. A little gnome of a woman, face creased like a prune, her toothless mouth bunched into a little round opening like a cat's behind. She sat on the stairs, feathers covering her hair, her pinafore and resting thickly on her eyelashes, stuffing them into a clean ticking bed cover from one slightly soiled.

'Madge,' said Eliza. 'Why are you shifting the feathers? It's scarce a year since they were all done.'

'Missus wants this house clean, she says, right down to the last feather. It's for the do.'

'The do! They won't be coming to look at the beds,' said Eliza.

'Well, you'd better get on and help,' replied Madge. 'Missus is right arty. Her frock's late and some of the taffeta has come up a different colour blue, and some of the fruit cakes have burned on top. She blamed Ruby for

91

stoking up the oven too much – hey, what are you laughing at?'

Eliza had started to giggle. Soon it gave way to helpless laughter. 'You don't half look funny with feathers round your eyes,' she gasped. 'You look like a caterpillar with birds' feathers.'

'That's daft,' scowled Madge, and her button mouth screwed up tighter.

'I know it is, but I feel better for that.'

It proved to be quite a pleasant day, spent upstairs in the bedrooms. She could hear old Madge grunting on the landing as she filled the feathers into the fresh covers, occasionally humming a tuneless tune. Down in the street, now and then, came the clip-clop of horses' hoofs. Once a hurdy-gurdy. Mid-afternoon, the cries of the muffin man.

Methodically, Eliza went from bed to bed, removing all the linen, darning holes, patching sheets, and sewing on new tapes.

Besides sheets, each bed had a fresh white cover for the feather bed. An embroidered valance trimmed with coarse lace was tied with tapes to each side of the bed. Bolster cases, pillow cases were renewed. So were the toilet bags hanging on the bed knobs where the ladies deposited their terry towelling diapers for her to wash.

On the dressing table hung embroidered bags stuffed

with hair when they cleaned their brushes. Toilet sets of white cotton and lace covered every part of the dressing table. On the marble-top washstand sat another set of covers made of terry towelling trimmed with a wide crochet frill.

That night in the pub Eliza got drunk. It was the only way she could find any ease from the pain in her legs. As always, Bill was busy with games of dominoes and exchanging loving glances with Ada.

When Ada was bold with drink, she rose unsteadily to her feet. Going over to where the men were sitting, she stood behind Bill, and, sliding her arms around his neck, she bent and kissed the bald spot on the top of his head.

There was a drunken roar from the crowd, and Ada looked towards Eliza with a gleeful grin on her face.

❦

On the evening of the party, Herbert and Clara Soppitt were the first to arrive.

Eliza had been instructed to put the guests' coats in the little side room, and not to get any grease on them, mind. She threw the coats over the chaise longue, putting the hats and gloves on a small table in the corner.

Albert and Annie Parker followed closely behind the Soppitts. Ruby opened the door to them, she had been told to bob because it was a special occasion. But the sight of Annie in her cape and bird-filled hat made her burst out laughing.

'What's up lass?' said Albert Parker.

'It's such a joyful occasion,' said Ruby Birtle who had done very well at school and was a quick thinker.

'Take a look at this lot,' she whispered as she thrust the offending garments at Eliza who waited in the side room.

Eliza chuckled to herself as she examined the hat in the dim light of the little room, she slipped it onto her head and laughed outright at her reflection in the mirror. 'Poor birds,' she said to herself. 'Fancy dying for that.'

Before placing the hat on the side table, she shook it in case one of her lice had jumped onto it.

The company settled down in a businesslike fashion and attacked the food in the dining room.

It was a splendid spread doing justice to the occasion. There was roast pork, roast beef, stand pie, salmon and salad, trifle and jellies. Many kinds of tarts, sponge cakes, rich fruit cake and cheese. There was a large jug of rum to add to the tea and this made the conversation very lively.

Eliza took her stand near the sink and started the washing up. There was a flurry of comings and goings through the front door and Ruby kept her well supplied with information.

Once the bell rang repeatedly from the dining room so Eliza went to look for Ruby. There she was, bold as brass

talking to the young man who played the chapel organ.
It was common knowledge he was courting Maria Helliwell's niece, Miss Nancy.

Afterwards, when Eliza was back with her pots and
pans, Ruby excitedly flung open the door. 'It's going to be
in 't paper,' she said. 'They're here from *Yorkshire Argos* –
two of 'em, one's a photographer. He's called Ormonroyd
and he's gone out for a bit, but he's coming back later.
Anyway, they've all finished their tea and they're in t'sitting room jawing away, when the doorbell goes and it's
the young organist. The women have all gone upstairs
now,' reported Ruby, 'and the men are in t'sitting room
having some sort of a row with the organist.'

Eliza opened the door into the hall and peered out.
The door to the sitting room was open a crack. She crept
forward and pressed her ear near the opening. She heard
some very strange things.

The young organist was reading a letter which seemed
to arouse a great deal of consternation and dismay, finally
leaving the three men who were celebrating their wedding anniversaries in a rather confused state.

It appeared that the parson who officiated at their mar-
riages twenty-five years ago had not been authorized to
do so. That being the case, none of them were married.

Oh, what a joke. All that carry on and they were not
even married.

Eliza stuffed the tea cloth into her mouth to stop her laughter. She shook silently with mirth outside the door.

The women were playing cards as Eliza finished her work, so she had no choice but to disturb the three of them to ask for her wages. She swallowed hard and opened the door without knocking.

They were sitting round the card table in their new party frocks. The three heads turned to look as she entered, each wore an expression as if they could smell bad fish. Each one had a hand poised in the air, holding a card.

The image, and their complacency, burned into Eliza's mind as she advanced towards the table. She became agonizingly conscious of her battered clothes, the poor shredded coat, the wretched skirt underneath, the unbecoming remains of a hat with its tangle of unkempt hair underneath, her thin, hole-filled, water-soaked boots.

Most of all she was aware of her hands, rough and callused, with broken nails and black dirt ground into every line from the work she had to do.

No matter how humiliating, she needed to ask for her money.

To her horror, she was told by the haughty Mrs Helliwell that she was not required any more after tonight. There followed a murmur of approval from the other women, which only increased Eliza's anger. It rose to a height when they told her to pay for a broken plate.

She could contain herself no longer and burst out with the news that they were not married, but living in sin.

At first they tried to ignore her but, as she persisted, they listened in horrified silence, and once she had reduced them to a dumb, staring state she picked up her money and withdrew.

When she went back down to the hall she found Ruby Birtle with another visitor. It was the mayor.

'Look here, Mrs Northrop,' said Ruby. 'It's the mayor, in his chain of office an' all. He's brought some fish servers for the happy couples, but I reckon he's had a few too many, he can hardly stand up.'

Ruby propped the fat man up with all her might, but she was only a slight girl and he was leaning very heavily against her.

'I can't keep this up, Mrs Northrop, you have to help me,'Ruby gasped.'Besides, I've got things to do, will you take him in?'

'I'll help him to the side room. My word, he has got a belly full, hasn't he?'

'Aye, and he's got a big enough belly to fill an' all,' giggled Ruby, and dashed off

Eliza took all the mayor's weight as he flopped across her shoulders. Stumbling slightly, she pressed him through the door into the side room. Sweeping the coats off the chaise longue she lowered the fat man on to it. His chain of office fell across his face.

'We'd better get that off, lad,' whispered Eliza and she flung the gold chain onto the little side table. Even in the fluttering gas light she could see he was a strange colour.

'Hey up lad,' she whispered. 'Reckon there's summat more than drink wrong with thee!'

Liquid was dribbling from his mouth and there was a strange rattling noise in his throat, occasionally an arm or leg would jerk violently.

'You need a bit of air, lad. You're a bit buttoned up. I'll loose you a bit.' And she proceeded to remove the lace around his neck, then started to unbutton his shirt.

'You've got your combinations on already, though it's only September, no wonder you're taken poorly, you're too hot.'

She continued to unbutton his shirt, then his underwear. Sweat was running down his bloated body, he was covered with ginger hair and had a strong body odour.

Soon her fingers touched something hard and she realized he was wearing a corset. It was extremely tight and cutting hard into his flesh.

'No wonder you can't breathe with that around your belly.' She grasped the clasps down the front to release the corset. As she opened it, his belly fell out in great pale folds of fat, quivering gratefully to be released.

She dragged the garment away from him and examined it in the light. What a handsome corset: black satin embroidered with tiny pink roses and a frill of black lace at the hem. It contained strong whalebones to hold in all that fat and make him an upright figure of a man.

Eliza was impressed when she compared it to her own pathetic undergarment of cheap cotton, holes, broken wire and bones digging into her ribs. This was a beauty.

Dropping the corset on the floor she leaned over the man. She lifted his shirt and wiped his face with it. When she looked at the fine white cotton, it was stained with make-up and the sweat had smudged the mascara around his eyes.

'Well, I never,' she said softly. 'Can you hear me, lad?' She gently pulled at his cheek but there was no response of any sort. The rattling had ceased and his eyes had opened a little way.

Eliza stopped and looked into his face. 'Well, old lad,' she said. 'I reckon you're going to need a couple of pennies for them eyes, I don't suppose it were drink that knocked you out this time.'

She spread her hand on his chest but there was a terrible stillness there. He was quite dead.

I'll leave 'em to it, thought Eliza and eased herself to her feet. She looked down at the corset on the floor. 'I've never seen owt like that,' she whispered. 'Black satin and roses, what would I give? But you won't need it any more, old lad, and you might be upset if folk knew about it. So you won't mind if I save you the shame, will you, old son?'

And with that she picked up the corset and put it in her bag under the beer bottles.

'He's just having a lie down,' she called to Ruby as she slipped out of the door.

Chapter 2

Eliza felt exhausted after such a momentous day. She decided not to go to the pub that night; it was getting late anyway.

George was sitting at the table when she arrived home. He was pressing leaves between sheets of paper, later on he would draw them. He stood as she came in. 'Hello, Mam. You don't half look tired. I've got a fire going. It's quite warm, come and sit down.'

As always, when anyone showed her any kindness or gentleness, tears pricked in her eyes. Usually, the world was so harsh as far as she was concerned that she had built a strong barrier around her. A word of kindness made that barrier crumble. A loving touch would have reduced her to dust. She lowered her head so he should not see her tears.

'Kettle's boiling. Do you want some tea or should I heat the poker for a glass of beer?'

'I'll have the beer, love,' she said, and with that he busied himself with pouring a glass of beer, heating the poker in the glowing fire, then plunging it into the beer

LIZ SMITH

until it foamed. 'By heck, that's good,' said Eliza as she drank.

She took off her soggy boots and warmed her feet by the unusually bright fire. 'It's been quite a day today, I needed that drink.'

'It was the do today, wasn't it? How did it go?'

'A day full of happenings.'

And she proceeded to tell him of all the dramas that had happened in the Helliwell household.

'Are you sure he was dead?' said George, when she told him of the mayor.

'Pretty sure. I let them get on with it, otherwise they'd have had me there all night, laying him out.'

'He lives with his sister.'

'Aye, Nellie. They still live in the house they were born in. But he owns a lot more beside that. He's a canny bugger.'

'I thought he was into all sorts of funny dealings.'

'Not half. Mean as hell, got his fingers into all sorts of pies. Hey up though, you'd better start tidying up, your dad'll be back soon and you don't want him to catch you drawing.'

George carefully laid his pencil down, he looked at her seriously. 'Mam,' he said. 'Me dad isn't coming back. Not tonight, maybe never.'

Suddenly she understood the fire, the care and

102

attention, and she despised herself for feeling sentimental. 'Oh, that's it. You've summat to tell me.' She spoke more harshly than she meant to.

'He told me to tell you, he's not coming back here. He's gone home with Ada. He's taken his spare pair of boots, and all his stuff, look.'

George indicated the table and for the first time she noticed the shaving mug and the boot iron had gone. Eliza stared at the table for a seemingly endless time as if it had something to tell her about Bill. She felt numb.

'Don't be too upset, Mam, we can pull together now. I'll do all I can for you.'

'Funny thing is, I don't feel anything much. Happen I won't think about it until tomorrow.'

They sat together for a long time. Each lost in their own thoughts.

Suddenly there was a sharp knock on the front window. It was Ruby Birtle on her way home, squashing her face up to the glass and laughing. 'I just thought you'd like to know, Mrs Northrop, what happened after you left.'

Eliza pressed her nose and mouth to Ruby's on the other side of the glass. They giggled together. 'Tell us,' she said. 'Tell us what happened.'

'Well, you can sleep easy tonight, because they are married after all. That Ormonroyd, that photo fella sorted it out for them. He was married at the same time by the same parson at the same chapel and he proved to them that they are married. So you see, it's all fine.'

'Well, Ruby, I reckon that's more than I am.'

'What d'you mean?'

'Bill 'as left me. He's gone off with Ada tonight.'

'You mean he's not coming back?'

'No. I wouldn't think so. Not never.'

Ruby fell away from the window in peals of laughter. 'Well I never. Well I never. What a turn up for the book that is. There'll be no more black eyes for you then, will there? Nobody to bruise your arms. Nobody to take your last penny for beer money. Poor old Mrs Northrop. No more Helliwells either. They don't want you back. You've a fresh start ahead of you tomorrow. Oh, and you know the mayor had to lie down in the side room, well they came and carted him away. He looked a goner to me. Anyway, ta-ra for now. Ta-ra.'

And with that Ruby set off skipping down the street.

Eliza kept her face pressed against the glass and watched her go. Bright little Ruby, barely sixteen, everything was such a laugh. She watched her dancing down the rough pavement and wondered what life held in store for her.

The fire had burned into a bright glow. With George now in bed, Eliza leaned back in the wooden chair, lifted her skirt and enjoyed the warmth on her legs.

As she moved, her feet caught her bag under the table. There was a clink of her beer bottles and she suddenly remembered the corset. She spread it out on the table to admire its beauty. She stroked the rich satin and the woven roses.

Fancy him having a lace frill around the bottom, she thought. Suspenders too. What sort of tricks had he been up to? she wondered, and smiled when she remembered the make-up on his face.

Nowt so queer as folk, she thought, as she lifted the garment to inspect more closely the workmanship, the rows of stitching, the quality of the fabric.

But why was it so heavy? She weighed the corset over her arm and could not understand it. Anyhow, it was much too big for her in its present state, she would have to take a large slice out of it; luckily she was handy with a needle.

Spreading it out again, she decided to remove a whale-bone on either side of the lacing, along with the surrounding fabric. The old kitchen scissors proved hopeless against the hem, she had to use the carving knife. Even the thin steel blade had difficulty in making the first cut. It seemed impossibly hard.

Eventually, she was rewarded with a small cut across the hemline. She gnawed away at the opening with the scissors and felt them touch something which seemed like metal.

Some kind of weight, she decided. Usually they were lead, but this stuff was a lighter colour.

Between knives, scissors and an old screwdriver, she extracted the first piece of weight. It was a golden sovereign.

How did that get in there? she wondered. It must have got mixed up with the lead ones. Let's have them out.

Now she worked with a will, tearing away at the fabric with anything that came to hand. Gradually the weights emerged, each one a golden sovereign.

Eliza was now inflamed with the complete destruction of the corset. She lashed at it with the scissors and knives. She stabbed it, she tore it, she unpicked obstinate stitches around the whalebones and hooks.

A pile of golden sovereigns had emerged from the hem, they gleamed in the gaslight. Eliza pushed them aside to count later, for she was determined to inspect every little piece of the shredded corset; she guessed there might be secret places in other parts besides the hem.

She was right. Underneath the satin trim by the steel stays down the front of the garment were six carefully folded notes, each to the value of one hundred pounds.

Her hands trembled as she counted – seven hundred and fifty pounds.

She did not stare long in amazement for Eliza was a practical person. She quickly decided to put the money into an old pillow slip and push it between the hard flock mattress and the broken steel spring of the bed. But where to put the pieces of corset? Not in a dustbin, they might be found and arouse suspicion. Besides, she must keep them in a secret place to go through again in case she had missed something.

She decided the safest place would be under a loose floorboard in the bedroom where she had occasionally stowed the odd shilling away from Bill's beady eye.

She curled up as usual on her side of the bed, then suddenly realized that Bill would not be there to claim his larger share. She rolled over to the centre and stretched her legs in a new sense of freedom. But before she had time to analyse it, she was asleep.

The following day Eliza was awake as usual at six o'clock, but lay still for a moment with a feeling that something was different. She put out her arm in the darkness. Bill was not there. She got out of bed and felt underneath the mattress. There it was, the old pillow slip containing seven hundred and fifty pounds.

So it was true; it *had* happened. Bill had gone and she was free to be her own mistress. What should she do now?

She went downstairs to brew a large mug of tea. She had a lot to think about. She could think about it all day. Today she was washing down the paintwork for old Mrs Stone, who was deaf as a stone. A quiet house and a quiet job; she could think and think about everything.

On her way out of the door, she turned back and stuffed the pillow case down her corset. After all, he'd kept it in his; it was a safe place.

All day as she worked, she kept touching the bulky package pressed next to her skin. Once she locked herself in the wash house and counted it. It was all there. It was all true.

Now then, Liza, she told herself, let's work this out. Whose money is it anyway?

It had been the secret hoard of Sam Moxton, Mayor of Clecklewyke. Sam Moxton who was well known to be in on any deal, no matter how shady, that would bring him money.

What if she was to take the corset and the money to the police station and own up?

Eliza shrivelled with fear at the thought of it. She would be in a prison cell before she could say Jack Robinson. What hope had she, a poor working woman, against the law? She might get years and years in jail for all that money, the rest of her life even.

She would send it anonymously. Drop it in quietly when no one was looking. Let it be found, but it would be as plain as the nose on your face that it was her.

Who else had been with him in the little room? Who else had loosened his clothing when he was fighting for breath? All his buttons were undone when they carried him away, only one person did all that – Eliza Northrop.

She knew that Nellie, his sister, would be well catered for. She decided to borrow the money.

On her way home the newspaper boys were announcing that the Mayor of Clecklewyke was dead.

No longer could she pay her nightly visits to the Hare and Hounds. She could not face sitting there seeing Bill and Ada, everyone knowing they were together and that she was now on her own.

She took a jug to collect some beer from the off-licence and treated herself to a nip of gin. She had black pudding for her supper, a pig's foot, and an oven-bottom cake of fresh bread, washed down with plenty of beer, then she built up the fire and settled down to think what she should do.

She had scarcely thought of Bill all day.

She looked around the dismal room: the bobbing light from the broken gas mantle, the dark smell of dry rot and the steady drip of water into buckets, the damp towel by the shallow sink with a smell all of its own.

That was the first thing she must do. Get another house. She could buy one. Tomorrow. A new one. Maybe with a proper kitchen and her own water closet. Perhaps it could have its own back yard, even a bit of earth where George could plant a few seeds.

She was so excited by the idea she felt she could rush out and buy one that very night.

But, wait a minute, Eliza, she admonished herself. Stop a minute and think. Supposing you, a poor scrubber from the back streets, turned up with a fistful of money and wanted to buy a house. Just what would everybody say? If you went with the money to the bank, the manager would call you into his office and want to know where the money had come from.

She felt paralysed as if she did not have the money at all. She had no background, no bank account. For her to produce any money at all would arouse suspicion. She had to go very slowly. She decided she must first find a better house to rent.

The first thing she bought was a sewing machine. George was surprised. 'That's a lot of money, Mam,' he said.

'It's from the tally man,' she lied, 'and I'll earn it back. As I'm not going to the Helliwells, I've decided to look for some sewing for that day.'

She found some sewing at the hospital. She took sheets, shrouds and bed shirts home with her and returned them neatly sewn. It paid more than the housework and was kinder to her hands. She soon decided to drop more housework and take on more sewing.

On her journeys back and forth to the hospital she looked for houses to rent. She still kept the money in her corset and she touched it regularly for reassurance. Pity she couldn't tell George, but he would benefit anyway without needing to know she had done anything.

She soon found a nice little terrace with houses to let, up in the streets by the hospital. The notice said, 'Please apply to McDuff & Kinley, solicitors.' She did, but not before she decided to buy a new hat. She found a good black velour one. It was cheap, respectable, but dull. It sprang to life, however, when she added a band of blue velvet ribbon. Her ragged working coat had fallen to pieces and was replaced by a second-hand, anonymous tweed.

She now felt she looked a decent enough citizen to apply to rent a house.

McDuff & Kinley had offices in an older part of the town; there was a quietness and an air of self-assurance about the area which made her feel nervous.

In the dust- and paper-filled interior she spoke in whispers, as if she were in church. She felt afraid; it was all so strange to her that she felt that she must be doing some unknown wrong, something that was obvious to anyone else but had never before entered her experience.

She froze with terror when she was shown into the office of Mr McDuff. He noted this and was kindly towards her.

'I would like to rent one of them houses please.'

'Now, Mrs Northrop,' said Mr McDuff. 'I have to satisfy the owners that you will be a reliable tenant, won't get into debt, will maintain the place in a proper manner. The first thing I must impress upon you is that the rent for this house is seven shillings and sixpence per week. Now, Mrs Northrop, tell me what rent you are paying for your present home.'

'Four and six,' she whispered.

'Ah well then, yes, you see, Mrs Northrop, this rent is a great deal of money. It is three shillings more you have to find every week, how can you guarantee that?'

'I know I can. I have a sewing machine now and I do less of the housework and more of the sewing jobs.'

'But surely they cannot pay all that well.'

'No, but I work long hours.'

'I believe you, Mrs Northrop. I believe you.' Mr McDuff noted her poor work-worn hands and the pleading in her eyes. He remembered his own mother who had scrubbed floors that he might go to study law, and his heart melted towards her.

❦

Eliza moved into James Street the following Easter. The cold, crisp weather gave her energy and a sense of elation.

She gave George his instructions. 'Hire Harry's horse and cart. Pack everything on to it, then go and dump it somewhere.'

'Dump it, Mam?'

'Aye, dump it, but don't let anybody see you.'

'Have you gone soft in the head, mam? How can we manage without a chair to sit on? Let alone keep up with all that rent. It's seven and six a week, Mam. Seven and six a week.'

'We're having new stuff,' said his mother. 'Not new new, but good, second-hand new.'

'We can't afford it. It would cost a fortune to furnish a whole house.'

'Ah, well then, we're not really going to furnish a whole house. I'm leaving the front room for sewing. Anyway, happen we won't be there that long.'

'Where are we going?'

'We might move to a better house someday. Who knows? If I do enough sewing. No, we'll just have our bare needs, but comfortable. I'll tell you one thing, we're having new beds, horsehair. I've had enough flock full of bedbugs.'

'I'm speechless. I'm speechless, Mam,' groaned

George. 'What are you leading us to? I think a bolt from heaven is about to fall on us for doing such sins I do not know.'

'Is it such a sin to want a water tap to myself? And a water closet?'

'You what?'

'I dream about having a water closet, George, all to myself. Except you could use it too. Just for us, and to flush it and flush it. I'd clean it and I'd polish it. Just to be able to go when I wanted to and not to find somebody sitting there.'

'I didn't know you felt like that, Mam.'

Eliza said, 'Neither did I, lad. I must have all these pent-up feelings inside me, now they're starting to come out.'

'I wonder why.'

'You'll never know, love. Maybe it's me having the change of life.'

Eliza brooded to herself about this. She was beginning to feel a different person. She was beginning to feel more daring. Mainly this was because she no longer had the foreboding presence of Bill hanging over her, pouring scorn on every idea she had. There was no Bill to slap her about the face and shoulders if she should dare to think of doing anything else than the most menial tasks for others to provide his daily fare.

114

She could not deny that a huge weight she carried around her neck seemed to be lifting. She found herself thinking more hopefully. And there was always the reassurance of that packet of money sewn into her corset. That gave her confidence.

She had noticed a change in George as well. He collected more plants, more grasses. He pressed them carefully between sheets of paper and drew them in great detail, and was able to leave his papers lying all over the table because his father would not be coming home. In the months since Bill had gone, without realizing it, both mother and son were slowly lifting their heads.

Without acknowledging it to each other, without daring to think it, they were better off without Bill. But to speak it out loud would have been too disloyal.

Chapter 3

To start their life in James Street, Eliza acquired only the barest necessities. She bought a chair each, two beds and a table, all from different shops in different parts of the town so that no one might suspect she had come into money.

She had a good rag rug for the hearth and new lino on the floor with a red Turkish carpet pattern which gave the little parlour a warm glow. She bought a beaded shade for the gaslight and a wooden rocking chair to sit by the fire.

There was a scullery with a water tap over the sink and a small, brick-built boiler with a fireplace underneath. A nail on the wall held a zinc bath so that on wash day, with the boiler fire still glowing, they could sit and soak with some good red carbolic soap.

The first thing Eliza did when she arrived at the house was to light the fire. When it was burning well, she stood in front of it, took a pair of scissors and clipped off her hair, piece by piece, right down to the scalp. As she cut the hair away she slowly placed it into the centre of the flames. It was a ritual burning. The lice on the hair were the sacrifice. There was a slight smile on her lips.

She pulled back the flap which sucked the heat up, then she burned her old hat in the oven. She had pomade from the chemist to rub into her bald scalp and a small-toothed comb to clean it off. She worked the comb until her head was red and raw but shining clean.

When George walked in carrying a chair he was greeted by an apparition of his mother turning slowly towards him, the fire playing in the background, bald as an egg. He had to sit down quickly and Eliza made him some strong, sweet tea.

He groaned. 'Whatever next? How could you do it? You can't be seen outside like that. Kids would follow you in the street and throw things at you.'

She laughed. 'I can crochet myself a cap. And you'd better do the same yourself, we've finished with lice now.'

George said he would take the linen back and forth to the hospital until her hair grew.

Thus they settled down to a peaceful way of life together. Eliza spent most of her time with her sewing machine, under the window in the front room. Her other jobs she let go one by one. Wash days she stopped first of all. The misery of the whetstone floors, twisting her body to turn the wooden dolly in the tubs, and the hideous weight of turning the mangle were all torture to her aching back and her painful rheumatic legs.

She worked for deaf Mrs Stone until she died because it was a quiet house and the jobs were light. But the sewing took over more and more. And now George was carrying the stuff it left her with more time, so she decided to invest in a treadle machine.

Mr McDuff did not want her to be just a name to be called on for the rent and so required her to visit once a month, with the money. When he was not busy he would invite her into his office and offer her tea. He felt he needed to keep track of this woman. He admired the way she battled with life and he wanted her to succeed. Not a young woman, either. Why, she was quite old. She did not have the advantage of education, of contacts to bolster up her courage, so it must be only her own true grit and determination.

He told her of a firm needing outdoor machinists to make simple blouses. 'Can you do that?' he said.

'Of course, Mr McDuff,' replied Eliza. 'I'm getting good at sewing now.'

'There might be some better-class blouses soon, perhaps with a touch of embroidery,' said Mr McDuff.

She told George about the blouses as they sat in the little parlour drinking tea. She loved these moments together. Rocking gently in her chair she could feel the remaining money pressed into her side, as the fire burned patterns on her painful legs and George organized his plants and drawings which now dominated the little room.

Jam jars filled with grasses were everywhere, until it became an enchanted forest. Once he mixed some flour and water and pasted his drawing of a wild rose on the wall. Eliza did not mind, so he stuck up another and another until there was a frieze of flowers of the country-side. They smiled together, for they both realized that no bully of a man would come shouting through the front door and throw the treasures away.

'Well,' said George. 'I like the idea of the blouses. It will make a change for you, a bit of colour after all them white bed shirts. But,' and he looked up solemnly from his work, 'I'm not sure about the embroidered ones, after all, you've never done that, have you?'

'I've been thinking. Happen I could get a bit of help. Get some lass who is good with a needle to help me. Expand a little, do a few different things. It would be a bit of company for me as well.'

That was how Maggie Turner came to sit with Eliza in the front room. Maggie had a club foot and because of her disability had been taught fine embroidery and sewing by the nuns at her school.

She was old beyond her seventeen years and her thin,

pale fingers wrought beautiful patterns on the cloth. Every morning the sound of her heavy foot coming down the street made Eliza smile, for she was such pleasant company. And a hard worker. Between them they managed to turn out a great many garments.

All the work was organized by George who fetched, carried and did the books. Eliza would just have done the work and pocketed the money, but he insisted on writing everything down with the dates and goods that changed hands. He was showing himself to be surprisingly good at it.

The nagging pain of the rheumatism in her legs and back drove Eliza to seek the help of Alice Proctor, a herbalist who lived a few streets away from her old home in Sarah Street. It felt odd being back in that area after such a long time and she felt a stranger to the place.

Even her visit to Alice Proctor was odd for she had suggested some very strange things. Eat little or no meat, she had said. Eat a lot of vegetables, she had said. Rye bread, and cut out drinking except for the occasional glass.

Alice had given her a packet of herbs to make a tea with and had told her that when the pain was bad in her legs, she had to plaster her joints with raw cabbage leaves, held in place with an elastic stocking.

Eliza walked down the street in a dream. How could

she manage without meat? She would die. How could she eat a plate full of cabbage, swedes, parsnips and stuff like that? She wasn't used to it. As for the drink, well, it was second nature to her to fill her glass. She did not feel she had the strength to stop it.

What funny advice. She would have been better to find a doctor who would tell her that at her age rheumatism was something she just had to live with. Then she could go on exactly as before.

She kept her head low against the heavy downpour of rain. She scarcely heard Anna Bentley calling her name and was not aware of her until Anna's blotchy face was thrust into hers.

'Liza Northrop.' The voice seemed to come from a crack of thunder.

Eliza jumped. 'Oh, Anna. You made me jump.' They moved into a doorway against the rain.

'I haven't seen you at the pub for such a long time, Liza.'

'I haven't been there since the night Bill went off with Ada,' said Eliza. 'You wouldn't expect me to, would you, Anna? How could I sit there with them smirking at me?'

'I don't think Ada's smirking now, Liza, Bill's off with another lass, Ada doesn't see much of him.'

'Serve her right, way she behaved with me, showing

off with Bill, but I expect she's set her cap at somebody else then. Ada's a great flirt.'

'She doesn't get much chance now she's stuck with a baby, and from what I hear, it's a sickly little thing.'

'She asked for it,' said Eliza. But after she had left Anna, she turned back and shouted, 'Where does Ada live now?'

'Next to the tripe shop in Charlotte Street,' came the reply.

A few weeks later she found her footsteps going in that direction. Enquiring for Ada, she was shown to a shabby little room where a pale, drawn version of vibrant Ada opened the door. She gasped when she saw her visitor. 'You're the last one I expected to see.'

'I don't know why I've come. Maybe it's to see a bit more of Bill's work.'

The baby *was* a poor little thing, lying on a piece of torn blanket in a drawer. Apparently, Bill turned up now and then to give a few shillings for the child. She had a little help too from the charity board but for this small sum she had to go and stand humbly before the group of worthy citizens as they scrutinized her mercilessly. Without compassion they questioned her and finally, grudgingly, they allowed her a little weekly sum from the fund, on condition, they said, that she would be sensible and not drink it all away.

122

Eliza gave her five pounds and told her to buy a little pram to give the child some air. For Ada was too weak to carry him far.

Why should I bother to help her? mused Eliza. I have no love for Ada. But finally she had to admit to herself, after a lot of soul searching, that she was grateful to Ada for having taken Bill away, leaving her and George in peace.

Slowly and inevitably she was becoming a different person, growing with confidence.

After three years, her hair, now grown and still dark, was clean and shining, brushed into a low bun at the nape of her neck. Gradually the black furrows of dirt had disappeared from her hands. The pieces of hard skin from her constant labour had worn away and her hands were soft and smooth. They were never as delicate as a lady's hands that had never known toil, but groomed enough for Eliza to hold them before her in wonderment.

Chapter 4

Eliza came to realize that things happened in groups of two or three. Soon after seeing Ada she had need to call at the hospital to discuss an order for some sewing.

Matron was not in her office, but was somewhere on the wards, Eliza was told. Maybe in maternity. She was led there by the screams of women in labour and the thin cries of newly born babies.

The long room was full of shadows. Eliza peered down the row of beds looking for an attendant matron perhaps standing stiffly behind a screen. She walked a little way down the ward. Some of the mothers watched her.

There in the corner one mother leaned against her pillow with an air of sad hopelessness. Eliza's heart gave a great jump, it was little Ruby Birtle. Ruby, that cheeky, cocky, confident little maid at the Helliwells'.

'Ruby,' said Eliza softly.

The young head on the pillow turned slowly towards her. Eliza could see the terrible shadows and the sadness in her face. Ruby flung her arms around her and burst into tears.

'Whatever is it, love? Did your baby die?'

'Oh Mrs Northrop, I wish she had, she's so beautiful, I want her so much and they won't let me keep her. I went once too often up to Cleckley woods and they tell me I'm a sinner and must be out of my mind to carry on like that, so I'm not fit to have her.' The words came tumbling out, punctuated by great shuddering sobs as she clung in desperation to Eliza's arms. 'Get her back for me, Mrs Northrop. Get her back for me, you must, you must.'

Eliza rocked the sad girl in her arms and gradually sorted out the story.

Ruby had indeed gone once too often to Cleckley woods and had found herself pregnant to a married man. Her mother lived in a tiny house that was already too overcrowded with family. The hospital decided it must be adopted.

Ruby had begged and pleaded that she would work night and day to keep her baby, but the citizens on the board would not listen and considered her a suitable case for treatment.

Ruby had seen the child as they took it away from her. She had held her arms out imploringly, but was dragged roughly back by the nurses who had no pity for a girl who had sinned.

'She was so beautiful, Mrs Northrop. I want her so much. Can you speak to matron, you know her don't you? I can do no more. They're sending me away, you know. I'm a sinner so I'm to be put away, Mrs Northrop. Please come and see me, if you can find me, for I know I'll be going to some place far off.'

'Oh surely not,' said Eliza to the matron. 'I'll help the child to keep her baby. I'll keep my eye on her, don't send her away.'

Matron, cold as a tall, thin icicle, turned and snapped at her. 'Mrs Northrop, girls such as Birtle do not deserve any pity, none whatsoever. It's pointless speaking about the baby. She has been adopted by a good respectable Christian family, approved by the Church, and will have every chance to lead a worthwhile life.'

'And Ruby?'

'Birtle will go into an asylum tomorrow. For the rest of her life, if need be. We cannot have such irresponsible members in our society.'

'That's heartless.'

'It is the law of the land, Mrs Northrop.'

Eliza was deeply disturbed by the fate of Ruby Birtle. No matter how she tried, no one would tell her where the girl had been taken. She tried all departments, but shutters went up before her eyes. She was rendered helpless by the authorities and that was the end of it.

❀

'We can't manage in the front room any more, Mam,' said George one day. He had found a tiny chapel to rent nearly two miles away, but it had good light and was big enough to take cutting-out tables and four machinists.

It was quite a way from their home and Eliza pondered on this. Suddenly she knew it was time to buy her own house. Up by the chapel workroom they were building some pleasant little villas. She decided to buy one of those.

She had known Mr McDuff now for over three years and his confidence in her had grown. She knew that. She also knew that by now she could leave the purchase of the house to him and she would no longer be in an impossible position and under suspicion if she produced the money.

She opened the pocket sewn into her corset and took out two hundred-pound notes. The cash in the corset was shrinking because of the investment in the business which was now her income. Nevertheless, she always kept some money in her secret pocket. Never less than one hundred pounds, never more than two. Just to give her the confidence that in an emergency, she would never be thrown into the lion's den and never have to rely on the kindness of others.

Eliza approached life with caution. She made decisions with the air of one walking on thin ice, expecting it to crack at any minute, and deep within her was a little niggling feeling that things were going too well. She'd had no real setbacks since Bill had departed and she now had money behind her. Surely her luck would change, she thought.

&

In 1912, the chapel workshop opened and Eliza bought her first house.

George, with a lot of good advice from Mr McDuff, organized the workshop in fine style. One section was for the sole purpose of dress trimmings and embroidery, all done by Maggie Turner and one assistant. A cutter at the head table was in charge of the four women machinists. Eliza and George had a tiny office in a storeroom, with a telephone.

Eliza's dream had come true. She stepped into her own home and looked around. At last, she had a cosy parlour, a front room with plush furniture and a carpet on the floor, a bathroom where a geyser heated the water with a loud burst of flame, a separate kitchen and wash house, and a small walled garden at the back.

It was a narrow terraced house, shadowy at the back because it closely faced the house next door. But to Eliza it was heaven.

She wandered from room to room, turned on taps, laughing out loud when hot water came out. She sat by her bright fire in a comfortable padded chair and counted her blessings. She wanted to sit back contentedly, but somehow she could not.

No matter how much she felt she had reached her goal, vague feelings of unrest and premonition still crept over her. She had an awareness that something was waiting to happen.

Mr McDuff came to see them one day after work was over. Eliza was sweeping the floor, making a neat pile of the bits of fabric and cottons. Outside in the street the lamplighter came and made the gas flare up into light, casting reflections through the windows into the shadows of the little workshop.

Eliza made some tea, George went out and bought them fish and chips and they sat around in a cosy group.

'I hope you don't mind having fish and chips with us, Mr McDuff,' said George.

'George, my boy,' came back the reply. 'My grandmother gutted the fish on the dockside at Campeltown – it took a lot of hard work to turn me into a solicitor you know.'

Mr McDuff went on to congratulate George on the way he had organized the place. 'And now,' he said, 'I have seen you do this, I wonder if you are in line to try something bigger. I think you are.'

'How do you mean, Mr McDuff?' said George. 'I can't believe the way this has come together, it already seems so much.'

Mr McDuff cleared his throat and pulled out his pipe from his pocket. 'I was telling your mother about the state of Europe. There is a war in the Balkans, which sounds far away, but sometimes a stone thrown into a pool a long way off sends its ripples over to us. Things are getting very restless, and certain government departments are beginning to make preparations. Not so as you'd notice, but in a quiet way.'

'Such as?'

'Such as armaments, food supplies and uniforms.'

'Uniforms? Is this place big enough for that?'

'It isn't, lad, that's what I'm getting at. I know you've just got here, but you would need a much bigger place. A proper factory. Why, this whole space would only do for the embroidery section, making the badges, the ornaments and the trimmings of rank etcetera, etcetera. It's a big job, would you like to have a go?' He looked at mother and son.

'If we could do it,' replied Eliza.

'Anybody can do anything they want to, especially you.'

'Well, thanks for your confidence, Mr McDuff, but as usual you'll have to tell us how to go about it.'

'For this one you'll need to see your MP.'

'It's Charles Dunne isn't it?' asked Eliza.

'That's right, I know him well. He has a surgery here once a month at the Bell Hotel. I'll make an appointment for you to see him, Mrs Northrop.'

Chapter 5

The Hon. Charles Theodore Crispin Dunne MP, second son of an earl, stood in front of the spotted mirror in the upstairs room of the Bell Hotel, Clecklewyke, and straightened his tie. He yawned and smoothed his hair.

Why, he wondered, were the upstairs rooms of pubs always so depressing? Every piece of wood had absorbed the smell of stale beer. The brown walls were backgrounds to the framed statements of various lodges. The curtains were always filled with grime and smelled strongly of smoke from the fire and generations of much-used pipes.

A waiter tapped respectfully at the door. 'Can I get you anything, sir?'

'Thank you, yes please. A pot of good strong tea, toast and marmalade.'

Charles thought he should fortify himself for his day. Meeting his constituents could be tiring, but it was the part of his work he felt most devoted to.

Harry Eden, his assistant, came to join him in his tea and toast and told him it was not a busy day. So far only five people had asked to see him.

❀

Eliza was overwhelmed at the idea of meeting an MP.
MPs were elected by the menfolk. They were remote. They
sat in the Houses of Parliament and talked endlessly,
deciding how the country should be run.

Eliza decided she needed an air of respectability;
otherwise he would never bother to consider her. She
needed to impress him, so had gone to Sheffield to buy a
new coat.

She'd chosen a long double-breasted coat of dark blue
faced cloth and a black hat of heavy velour with a single
black silk rose on the brim, a black skirt and a white blouse
caught at the throat with a small jet brooch that George
had bought for her.

'How do I look?' she asked him.

George looked astonished. 'Oh Mam,' he said. 'You look
just wonderful. I had no idea you could look like that.'

'Well thanks very much, lad, I'm glad my son has such
a high opinion of me.'

'I don't mean that, Mam, you know that, it's just that
nobody would have any idea that this woman had been
lurking inside the woman that was.'

She laughed. 'So you think I'll do?'

'More than that, Mam. I think you will get it.'

Eliza was very familiar with the downstairs of a pub,

but had never been in the upstairs rooms. Harry seated her to wait in a long, brown, shadowy corridor. There was a shabby piece of stained, once-red carpet on the floor, and walls that seemed to have a strange disease.

She could hear the low murmur of voices behind the door. On the chairs beside her were two men, each with a missing limb. One had a wooden leg. Crouching low, several chairs away, a man had distanced himself and was sobbing softly into his tear-stained shirt front. The door opened and out came the first applicant.

One by one they were called. By the time it was Eliza's turn she could scarcely stand, her heart was beating so wildly. She felt overdressed. She should have chosen just plain, dark, respectable clothing. He would dismiss her straight away. The tension showed on her face as she entered.

The discussion went ahead in a very stilted way. There were awkward silences and they seemed to be making little progress.

The ever-helpful Harry sensed Charles's tiredness and suggested a cup of tea.

'What a good idea, Harry. A short break will do us good. It's been a long morning and Mrs Northrop would enjoy one I'm sure.'

So, here she was, in the upstairs room at the Bell, drinking tea along with her MP.

Eliza used her cup to conceal her sly glances at the man. His tweed suit was of a cut not often seen in Clecklewyke; his gold watch chain led into his waistcoat pocket and on it was a heavy gold seal; his brown leather shoes shone like glass; she noted his socks were silk. As to his face, she had no idea. She did not dare look as far as that. For the time being she was satisfied to look no further than the knot in his tie.

Harry carried the situation along with chat about the weather. As she turned her head, Charles took a quick look at the woman. His eye was drawn to the flash of white blouse at her throat, and the heavy bun of dark hair in the nape of her neck.

'Mrs Northrop,' he said. 'This is too complicated to resolve today. I am here again two weeks today. Will you come back?'

She rose with a faint sigh of relief and was glad when she was out in the street. She did not know why, but she took the wrong turning on her way home.

'I don't like the sound of this, Mam,' said George later. 'Sounds a bit fishy to me. I think he's got other plans. What was he like anyway?'

She hesitated. 'Do you know,' she said with a surprised look, 'I didn't really see him. If I was to meet him in the street now, I wouldn't recognize him.'

A few days later she was given a pass to visit Ruby

Birtle. It had been very difficult tracing her and even harder to get permission to see her.

Eliza went on the train, which stopped at a tiny station seemingly in the middle of nowhere. From there a horse-drawn cart picked up the few visitors to the institution. They sat on hard benches rattling along over the stony road in complete silence. They formed a sorry little group carrying offerings wrapped in newspaper for the unfortunate souls they were to visit.

The grim buildings rose up before them like the wrath of God – an edifice of doom set in the endless rolling countryside of the mist-filled moors.

It must always be raining here, thought Eliza. The sun would never shine on this place.

A woman of manly appearance and strong moustache directed them to an area to look for friends. Ruby was to be found in the garden.

Eliza walked tentatively down a corridor which led outside. The floors and walls shone with a green glow. There was a strong smell of disinfectant and urine.

In the garden, Ruby was nowhere to be seen. Just a few bedraggled privet hedges and an occasional wooden seat.

Eliza wandered around, and, following a rough stone wall, found it developed into a covered bench. It was almost a cave. At the back, behind a curtain of ivy, crouched Ruby Birtle.

'Whatever are you doing, Ruby?' Eliza sat beside the girl. 'You're not hiding from me, are you, lass?' She took the frail little form in her arms and rocked her.

Ruby let out a shuddering sigh. 'Oh Mrs Northrop, I'm finished. You know, I didn't want to see you. I didn't want you to find me. I didn't want anyone to find me ever, ever, ever. I'm done. They've made me the same as them.' She looked around her like a creature in a trap.

They sat for a while, silently taking in the sad scene, and in that brief moment Eliza felt separated from the world. The heavy mist, drifting more thickly, now had cloaked the top of the moors with dark clouds. The wandering paths disappeared into hidden hills which were then enveloped by moving wetness.

'Is it always like this?' asked Eliza.

'Aye, it is. I think it's the moors. I think they pull the clouds down.'

'Can't do you any good.'

'It doesn't.' Ruby leaned her head wearily against Eliza's arm.

'Where's your spirit, love? Where's that cheeky auld lass I knew? A little fighter she was.'

Ruby kept her eyes closed. 'She's gone, Mrs Northrop. There's just me in her place. I haven't the strength anyway. You should see the food in here. It's pig swill. I only have enough energy to think about Imogen. Imogen, that's what I call her, Mrs Northrop. Imogen. It's out of a play by Shakespeare. We did it at school. I always said if I had a little lass I'd call her Imogen. I think it's a lovely name. Look at it written down.' She pulled a piece of creased paper out of her pocket. It was headed IMOGEN. On it were all the details of the child's birth, time, weight and progress. The first tooth. The first smiles of recognition.

'I think about her all the time, Mrs Northrop. I tear at the blankets in the night and wake screaming, longing for her. Sometimes she is so real I think she must be in bed beside me, but when I reach out it is only the pillow.'

Eliza was silent. She knew the agony.

'I'm so young, Mrs Northrop. I've got a whole lifetime of this, for I can see nothing but being here in this prison for the rest of my life. I must stay here and make note of every birthday. When she goes to school, when she is married. I may even be a granny someday. But she will never know I exist, and I love her so.'

Eliza spoke slowly. 'I wish I could say something to you, love. But I'm flummoxed.'

They sat together like stone figures in the shadow of the dark ivy, eyes fixed on the sad landscape. Eventually, Ruby spoke. 'I wish my last day on Earth was tomorrow.'

Eliza stirred. 'Not really, love. If only we could get you out of here, you'd have some fight left in you. I know you'd manage better if you were back in the world outside.'

The leaving bell rang.

Eliza rose. 'I'll do all I can.'

The bell rang again.

'Oh I forgot. I brought you a fruitcake.'

From her cart back to the station, Eliza watched the ever blacker clouds descend on the wild and lonely moors. She twisted her head to catch a last glimpse of the place. Rain trickled down her face. On her lips she tasted salt where the rain mingled with her tears.

❀

It was requested that on her second visit to Charles Dunne MP she should be accompanied by George. This time she removed the black silk rose from her hat, putting a ribbon in its place. George looked respectable and tidy in his navy blue suit, as befitted a man in partnership of a firm to make clothing for the armed forces.

Harry greeted them. Eliza was pleased to see him again.

The meeting was brief. It was agreed they should go ahead with the arrangements. George and Harry were to look at suitable premises, then there would be further meetings. Charles hardly spoke; most of his remarks were addressed to George, which gave Eliza the opportunity to observe him without seeming rude. He was not good-looking, but handsome in the way he held himself with an air of complete self-assurance. He was above average in height, his grey-blue eyes made no allowance for liars. Rather stern in repose, his face radiated kindness when he smiled.

Eliza began to relax in her chair and found she was looking at him rather than listening to him. When the meeting was over, Charles opened the door for her. 'No black silk rose today?' he said.

Surprise shone in her face. 'Next time,' she said. 'Next time.'

They went to inspect an empty cotton mill on the edge of town and in her hat she wore the black silk rose. The party consisted of Eliza and George, Charles, Harry and Mr McDuff.

The stone mill stood pale against the surrounding countryside. The moors rose up behind the building and down the slope of the road were rows of tiny workmen's cottages. It was small as mills go, but just the right size for them.

The sky shone brightly behind the mill as they arrived, but by the time they had looked around, a sharp wind had blown up and was spitting rain. Charles shuddered.

'It's bleak,' he said. 'Let's find something to eat. Is anyone interested?'

They all agreed and went to their waiting horses and traps.

Eliza felt her stomach tighten, she realized they would be going to a restaurant. Please God don't let me trip over my skirt. Don't let me drop all the knives and forks. Would the waiter be long-faced and disdainful? Would he sneer when she tried to tell him what she wanted?

Oh, pull yourself together Eliza, she silently admonished herself. You are a businesswoman deserving of respect, and if you don't know how to behave, you'll quickly learn.

The hostler took the horses and they went into the dining room at the Bell. The landlord settled them with great care and attention at a round table by the fire. A waitress was summoned to take their order, a comely woman, about forty years old, with ruddy cheeks and a comfortable, rounded shape. Her black skirts almost touched the floor and her frilly white cap and apron were immaculate. She gave a slight bob and asked for their order.

The men had steak and kidney pie. Eliza asked for steamed cod and parsley sauce, as she rarely ate meat nowadays. Afterwards they ate the landlady's excellent apple pie. Charles ordered wine, and as she sipped it in the firelight, Eliza felt suddenly relaxed and happy.

Charles noted this as he continually felt his eyes drawn towards her sitting in the lamplight, rather nervously fingering her glass, her blouse softly white, and the black hat sometimes casting her face into shadow.

'Like it or not,' said Charles, 'we will have many such meetings. With Mrs Northrop and her son at the head. We must be the support behind them.'

'We couldn't manage without you,' replied George. And Eliza had to agree.

From then on life became a whirl of activity. One morning, George even forgot to eat his breakfast.

'What's up with you, lad?' his mother enquired. 'You're rushing about like a penny kite.'

'I can't believe it's happening, Mam. I'm learning every day.'

So the setting up of the factory went on, one step after another, until it was complete and ready to begin operations.

Eliza felt she could hardly breathe. Every day she expected disaster, to hear the news that the whole thing had collapsed, but no, nothing went wrong. The orders came in and they advertised for workers.

Charles Dunne was happy with his part in the setting up of the factory. It was a diversion, an adventure. After all, someone had to have the tender for the stuff. Why not this mother and son?

He told the story to his wife Lydia. She listened with delight. All stories were grist to her, but this was a good one. 'It's so exciting, Dodo. What an adventure for them. How very daring of them. And the woman isn't very young?'

'No, she is my age,' said Charles.

'You're old, Dodo,' cried Lydia and burst into peals of laughter, knowing that she was six years his junior. She was still playful and pretty, even though she had scarcely left her room for the last twenty years.

A hunting accident had developed a wasting disease in her spine. She eagerly awaited her visitors and begged them to chatter on, to bring life to her. Especially Charles, and she insisted on his supper being brought to her bedside instead of served in the dining room.

'Describe them to me, Dodo,' she would cry. 'Act them out for me.'

And he would amuse her with his imitations of the people he had met that day. For he was a good mimic and very observant.

Although Lydia left her room only on rare occasions, her life was not lonely, for she had Charlotte as her daily companion. Charlotte, her niece, was a spinster, thirty-five years old and extremely plain. She lived in the manor house bordering onto the estate and took it upon herself to manage the gardens for herself and her aunt.

One afternoon, the talk around the fire with Aunt Lyddie flowed freely. The two main subjects were the gathering war clouds in Europe and this ordinary working woman who, with her son, had been bold enough to apply for tender to make clothing for the armed forces.

'It does sound extraordinary,' said Charlotte. 'It's usually a committee of men who decides these things; she must be a strong character.'

'Or so ignorant of the task, she steps into it blindly, a case of where angels fear to tread.'

'Is she totally ignorant?'

'No not quite. Apparently she has had a small sewing business in her front room for a few years, you know the way they do, open the front room as a shop in extremity. They have just moved to a small chapel premises, but that alone can't take them to the next big step.'

'Someone else must be putting money into it,' mused Charlotte.

'I rather think Charles is,' said Lydia slowly.

'I would like to see this woman. What is her name?'

'Mrs Northrop. Yes, so would I. Lottie, your next horticultural tea, instead of your place would you have it here, for me?'

'And invite Mrs Northrop?' Charlotte raised her eyebrows.

'Yes.'

144

'Yes, Aunt Lyddie, I'd like to do that.

'Invite the son too. Let's have a real feast.'

'Wouldn't that be a waste of time?'

'I'm sure it would, by all accounts he looks like a cold suet pudding, and probably can't think any further than buying a few yards of cloth at a knock-down price, but still I'm curious to meet him.'

'I'll organize it.'

❀

Eliza stood on the platform outside the office windows, leaning on the iron rail, looking down at the factory floor. This was hers. Not hers alone, of course; there were George, Charles and Mr McDuff, all supporting her as well. Nevertheless, it was like a dream. She could not believe how it had all come about.

Of course, she'd had the freedom of some money in her pocket and the still greater freedom of having the dead weight of Bill lifted from her shoulders. But that wasn't enough to account for her being here today. Why did these people support her, when in the past she had met no one who did not want to put a boot in her face and grind her down into the ground with their heels?

It could not continue. She was sure she would get her comeuppance for 'borrowing' that money.

She raised her arms above her head to ward off the

LIZ SMITH

imaginary blows her fearful mind conjured up. To quell
her beating heart she took a glass of the sherry she kept
in her office, then went down the steps to sweep the factory floor.

'Don't you do that, missus,' said Eli the nightwatch-
man, coming out of the shadows. 'That's my job.'

'We talk about this every night, Eli. I've just got to do
it, to mark the end the day. You can do it again when I'm
gone, make sure it's done properly, but it is just my habit,
you see. I've worked hard all my life and I can't stop it. I
don't suppose I ever will.'

'There's work and work, though, missus. You don't
need to sweep the floors.'

'Yes Eli, I do need to.'

'Have it your own way, missus, you're the boss'; and
he drew out of his pocket a torn and dirty handkerchief
and wiped his ugly nose.

Eli was a remarkably ugly man altogether – in fact, his
appearance was quite repellent. A huge man, his big red
hands emerged from his jacket like a bunch of tropical
fruit hanging down. His face was drawn into a terrible
leer by the ill-healed scars he'd received from the Boer
War. And the wound he had received at the relief of
Mafeking ensured that his tall body would always lean
on a spiral.

His strange and fearsome appearance made it

impossible for him to find work and he felt an immense loyalty to Eliza for employing him.

Moreover, he had more than one reason to feel grateful towards Eliza. His niece Ada was the same Ada who had borne a sickly boy to Bill. Ada was a silly bitch of a woman, and no better than she should be, thought Eli, but he loved her and she was growing old now. Nobody helped her much with that strange little boy, except Eliza.

'I'm off now Eli,' called Eliza as she left the factory.

'Don't worry, missus, I'm here.'

She stepped out into the night. It would do her good to walk home; she needed the exercise and the fresh air. First, she went a short way up the road to look behind the building and there, stretching out forever, were the moors, windswept and menacing.

A bright moon almost obscured by the scudding black clouds painted a pale outline on the rugged hills and deep ravines, making the shadows even darker. Eliza shuddered as she looked upon it. She felt as though she were in some strange, alien land and the dark pathways led to terrors unknown.

Even as she stood there, the wind grew stronger, the clouds swung more violently across the moon, and the few scraggy trees leaned further to the ground.

She was glad to turn and make her way down the little

cobbled streets which would take her into the dip of the town, and home. But she took with her an awe-inspiring feeling of fear, as if she were standing on the edge of an abyss.

Chapter 6

When Eliza arrived home her spirits revived at the sight of her own front door and by the time she had settled into her cosy armchair in front of the glowing fire she felt content with the world again.

George cooked a supper of baked haddock and mashed potatoes, followed by Bramley apples cooked in the oven until they burst, with brown sugar and cream.

Afterwards they drank tea laced with whisky, and George wound up the gramophone. He turned the great horn into the room and in the lamplight and fire-light floated the music of Irving Berlin and Franz Lehár.

Eliza went contentedly to bed, and fell asleep with a smile upon her lips.

The next morning the postman brought a letter. Eliza stood staring down at it as it lay on the mat.

'George,' she called. 'George, come and look here, there's a letter on the mat.'

'Perhaps it's the gas bill.'

'No, it's not a bill. I can see it's a letter.'

George came down into the hall. 'Well then, aren't you going to pick it up?'

'It can't be for me, I've never had a letter before – bills yes, lawyers' stuff yes, and they all go to the factory. But not a proper letter.'

'Well, if you won't pick it up, I will. Anybody would think it was a spider. Here you are, it's written in a very nice hand.'

Eliza propped it against the milk jug and scrutinized it as she ate her toast and marmalade. She had to agree with George, it was written in a very nice hand, and on very good paper.

George was busy in his little garden, saying good morning to his flowers, when his mother joined him with the opened letter.

'You'll never guess. You'll never guess, lad. We are invited to the summer meeting of the Horticultural Society, with a tour of the gardens at the hall. It is signed Charlotte Holmes. Now what do you think to that, then?'

'Who is Charlotte Holmes, Mam?'

'She is the niece of Charles Dunne's wife.'

'She interested in plants?'

'She practically runs the two estates – her own and Charles's place.'

Eliza visited Sheffield again to buy a suitable outfit. She chose a long jacket and skirt in cream shantung silk, a white silk blouse with lace at the neck and a large hat of fine cream-coloured straw, edged with black velvet ribbon. A handbag of black velvet embroidered with cream silk flowers, especially sewn for her by Maggie in the workroom, completed the outfit, which she hoped would not look too grand.

The day of the flower show dawned brightly. It was hot by ten o'clock in the morning. Eliza felt too warm in her jacket when she climbed into the trap. George gently touched Kitty the horse on her flank, and they were off.

The bell on Kitty's harness rang softly with the clip-clop of her hooves and soon they were driving along wooded lanes which dappled them with sunlight.

Away in another country, a visiting archduke took a ride in a carriage, but his flowers contained a bomb. Unaware of this, George and Eliza went along their way.

'Don't go too fast, lad,' she said. 'Go slowly, I'm enjoying it.'

'Shall we take the long road round, Mam?'

'Why not, we've plenty of time.'

And so, thanks to that decision, Eliza found the house of her dreams – a beautiful, homely, handsome house, set high, with lawns running down into shrubs and trees.

Eliza gazed at it with eyes of wonder, it was just what she had always dreamed of. And look, there was a notice board which read: 'FOR SALE'.

So deep was she in her reverie about the house, Eliza had no time to be shy at the gathering. She found herself sitting contentedly in the warm golden light of the marquee, drinking tea from a delicate china cup and chatting to the company as if they were long-lost companions.

Huge displays of roses and sweetpeas filled the air with perfume and the sweetness of the turf beneath her feet gave her a heady sense of well-being.

Lydia held court in the cool of the conservatory, lying on a chaise longue, wearing an exquisite Liberty gown. She was as lovely as any flower there. Eliza was quite startled by her beauty which seemed to be almost from another world. The silks and colours that surrounded her were such as Eliza had never seen before and they stirred her emotions. At the same time, Lydia was noting the quiet good taste of Eliza's cream suit.

So they examined each other as women will, and liked what they saw.

'You were a long time gone,' Eliza said to George, as they settled into the trap.

'I saw a lot more than you, Mam.'

'It was too hot for me, love. I didn't go far afield.'

'There were some lovely things, Mam. Plants I never knew existed. Some I'd seen in library books, but when you see them for real you can hardly believe it . . . and yet.'

'Yet what?'

'Well, it's a funny thing. All them amazing flowers, acres of them, all different, and do you know, the show-piece in the main hall was cow parsley.'

'That's a weed.'

'Aye, but you should have seen how it looked. Like lace. And smelled so sweet. Not put in a jar as you might expect, but a lovely pale-green vase! Chinese, priceless, Miss Holmes said. She knows everything about plants. She has her own great place, as well as this one. She says I must go and see it.'

'I see. Well, you did get on all right then, didn't you?'

'We got on like a house on fire.' And George tickled Kitty on her rump with the whip until she broke into a trot.

❀

'But you've only just moved into your present house,' said Mr McDuff as he polished his glasses again and again. 'This is a more expensive property altogether. I hope you're not getting frivolous in your old age.'

'I definitely am getting frivolous in my old age. Until something stops me.'

'What's going to stop you?'

'I don't know. But I always think it's just round the corner, everything that's happened lately has gone without a hitch. It can't be like that for ever.'

'You think your luck won't hold?'

'It can't. There must be a big disaster waiting for me somewhere round the corner. I just keep wondering what it will be, and when.'

Mr McDuff gave her a quizzical look over his glasses. 'You're an odd woman. But if you weren't, I don't suppose you could have done what you have done. In a strange way, events that are happening may pay for your house and a lot more. After that assassination in Sarajevo, Germany is invading Belgium. I am sorry to say, I think you will be getting a lot more orders for uniforms.'

❀

One day in August, Eliza was working her way through a pile of wallpaper patterns. George and Charlotte, on their first outing together, had gone to a concert by the Clecklewyke male choir. And Great Britain declared war on Germany.

By December, Eliza was standing in the drawing room of her new home, wondering where she should put the Christmas tree, when George brought in a tea tray. Along with the house, Eliza had inherited Alice and Ben to care for her, so it was Alice now who usually made the tea. Seeing George carry in the tray gave her a sudden sharp stab of premonition.

'Alice busy?'

'I don't know, I just felt like making us some tea. Sit down, Mam.'

There was a comfortable silence between them as she poured the tea. George watched his mother and mused how well she looked, still no grey in her dark hair.

Alice's cat ran through the door and jumped on George's lap, he stroked its back and found great pleasure in it. His life had never had space or time to contain animals, now he was beginning to enjoy contact with them. The cat purred loudly and the fire burned bright.

Eliza broke the moment. 'Well, come on then, what's on your mind? I know there's summat. I can feel it in my bones. Have you joined up?'

'They wouldn't have me. I've got flat feet and I'm making stuff for the war effort.'

'Well, thank God for that. I don't want a dead hero for a son.'

'Would you like a married son?' George went on to tell her that Charlotte had asked him to marry her.

Eliza leaned back heavily against the curve of the sofa, staring at him. 'Pull the other leg, it's got bells on,' she gasped.

'It's true, Mam, I can't believe it either. I keep waking up at night thinking I must have dreamed it, and then I remember, she did ask me.'

155

'What did you say?'

'I said yes.'

'Shouldn't it have been the other way round, doesn't the gent ask the lady?'

'By rights, yes, but she knows that I'd never get around to asking her. She's so far above me, I wouldn't dare, no matter how much I loved her.'

'And do you love her?'

'Oh yes, from the moment I met her I had this lovely glow. Well, you know what it feels like when you're in love.'

'No I don't. I've never been in love and I don't think anybody's been in love with me.'

'Didn't you ever love my dad?'

'No, we just rubbed along together. As for love, it just depended how much beer he'd got inside him.'

'Oh Mam, I'm sorry that nothing better than that has happened to you. I do know that I love Charlotte, and I really believe she loves me.'

'Well, I'm flabbergasted, I mean you're not much of a catch, are you? All the handsome men she must know from London and she picks on you!'

'She doesn't want to marry all them handsome men from London, she wants to marry me.'

'But look at you. You're nowt to look at. You're short and fat. Your skin is as pale as lard and you've got flat feet. Nobody could call you handsome.'

'Mam, go easy on me, after all I am your son.'

'You are that, and I don't mind telling you that I think the sun shines out of your arse, but that doesn't stop me seeing you as others might. Although, God help them if they said owt against you.'

Then followed a very happy time for Eliza. George and Charlotte planned to marry the following Easter. On Christmas Eve, Charlotte came to supper wearing her new engagement ring.

Alice rose to the occasion and baked a whole salmon. Ben wore his best black suit and opened the front door to the guests. Charles escorted Charlotte, and Mr McDuff brought his niece. It was all so easy and happy, Eliza did not realize that she was giving her very first dinner party.

Soon after ten o'clock, Charles suggested they went to the little church nearby, for the midnight service. Charles's coachman and Ben brought the respective horses and traps to the door. Charlotte wanted to ride with George, so Eliza rode with Charles.

It was a magic night. A thick white frost covered the town, making the most ordinary objects appear beautiful. A full moon bathed the scene in a pale light which caused every little speck of ice to twinkle and glitter. Every twig, every tree, shone silver. There was a stillness in the air which made the horses' hooves crack the silence.

Eliza, snug in Charles's carriage, heard the faint tinkle

157

of Kitty's bells on the road ahead, but could see nothing because the windows of the cab were curtained with ice.

For a moment they drove in silence. Then Charles slowly turned, and rolling back the top of her glove, kissed Eliza's wrist.

She looked at him and smiled. 'I've been hoping you'd do something like that for some time now,' she said. And with that he kissed her on the cheek, very softly, very slowly.

She had never been kissed like that and before she could stop them, the tears were sliding down her cheeks. All she had known was to be pushed down and jumped on and the very tenderness of this kiss broke her self-control. 'I'm not used to it,' she explained to him.

'So I'm not to kiss you again?'

'Oh yes please. I'd like to get used to it.'

He put his arms around her. He hugged her tight in the little cab with the ice-bound windows and the clip-clop of the horses' hooves.

When they left the church it was snowing and the golden light from the doorway spilled over the church-yard. The horses stamped and pawed the ground, eager to go. Everyone shook hands wishing each other a very happy Christmas.

Eliza had never known anything like it. Not only did it look like a picture on a Christmas card, but she had been in the heart of a church and included in the service. Over and above that, she had been kissed in the back of a cab by an MP, a man she admired more than she dared to admit.

In the first hour of Christmas day she stood in her nightdress watching her reflection in the dressing-table mirror. 'It's your best Christmas yet, Liza,' she said, and blew out the candles.

❀

The newspapers on New Year's Day carried an appeal for an extension of the children's ward built in memory of a former mayor of Clecklewyke. Eliza gave an anonymous gift of seven thousand pounds to the fund, and felt she had finally paid her debt. The many years of guilt over the money's origins were over. It was an enormous relief.

January was a dark month. There were battles in France with many dead. The snow lasted for weeks and turned black with soot, clinging to the pavements like mountain ranges. Horses struggled and slipped up and down the harsh cobbled streets, many beaten mercilessly.

There was a slight thaw towards the end of the month which turned the dirty snow into slush, soaking into clothing and straight through the thin soles of most of the townsfolk's shoes. Long icicles which had hung from every rooftop, and out of the frozen pipes at the back of the factory, now dripped, and Eli had been in and out all day with the plumber.

It was a messy business. Eliza had some good hard sweeping to do that night, especially by the outside door. It was a dark and shadowy area, and she was having trouble with some lumps of rag that had frozen to the floor.

A blast of cold air told her that the door had been opened. She peered into the gloom. 'Is that you, Eli?' she called. 'I'll have to leave this bit for you.'

'It's not Eli,' said a voice she had not heard for some time.

It was Bill, standing there in the shadows, hat at a rakish angle, tattered overcoat hanging in shreds, the moustache still tweaked up at the corners. 'Hello Liza.'

Her heart gave a sudden jolt. 'What do you want?'

'Just a friendly word, Liza, for old times' sake, you know.' He strolled jauntily past her and into the machine room. 'My, my, this is a bit of all right isn't it? I've heard all about it but had to see it for myself.'

'What do you want?'

'I want to come to the wedding. I'm told our George is making a very good match and I want to be there. After all, I'm still your husband.'

'I'd see you dead first.'

Bill thrust his grinning face into hers. 'By God, Liza, I like you when you're in a passion. I've never seen you like this. You've grown into a right handsome woman, I could fancy you, I could that.' His hand touched her arm.

She lifted the broom handle and leaned away from him. But she need not have worried. Two big red hands gripped him by the throat from behind, and towering above him, Eli lifted him high into the air, arms and legs beating.

Holding Bill up like a kitten, Eli asked, 'What shall I do with him, missus?'

'You can put him down, Eli, but stay within sight.'

Bill was cowed but not beaten. Glancing uneasily towards Eli, he hissed at Eliza. 'I'll not come into your lad's life. You can keep your fancy friends, but you'll pay for it. I need money. Look at me boots, done for, and the same with this coat in this weather. The only place I have to sleep on is somebody's floor.'

'How much?'

'One hundred pounds.' He spoke slowly and deliberately, a greedy gleam in his eye.

'Come back tomorrow night at the same time, I'll get it for you.' She had a leaden feeling in her stomach and an air of foreboding she could not shake off.

He was there as promised, the following night. The meeting was brief. She silently handed him the money.

He grinned, instinctively his arm started to move towards her, but stopped abruptly as he turned and saw Eli standing silently in the shadows.

Bill turned to go, but not before he fired his parting shot. 'I'll be back,' he said.

And she knew he would. He had found a source of income such as he had never known and Eliza knew she must play her part and pay up. She would do anything rather than have him enter their lives again, particularly for George.

She shuddered as she realized the disaster it would be for Bill to appear and confront his son under his new circumstances. Though George wasn't exactly a gentleman, he had a natural dignity which commanded respect and affection, and the appearance of a destitute and drunken father would harm his status.

For Bill, a new world had opened. He had an endless supply of money and complete freedom to do as he wished.

He frequently chuckled to himself. In fact, sometimes he stopped dead in the street, threw his head up and laughed out loud, which gave the impression to passers-by that he was not only a waster but off his rocker. With his new-found wealth he no longer had to stick to ale and stout but could drink spirits. He also used a better kind of pub that was a bit more plush and had a better class of prostitute.

With his new clothes, he felt he could go anywhere and make an entrance. He tweaked his moustache in pub mirrors and decided he looked a real toff in his brown bowler hat. The bowler added the final touch to his new overcoat, a full-skirted garment in a rather violent check pattern that was several inches too long for his little portly figure.

Best of all, he loved his new boots, two-tone and completely waterproof. Bill had never known what it was to have dry feet in a rainstorm.

There were moments when he considered finding a house for himself. But the moment soon passed. Why waste money on bricks and mortar now? That could come later. Better to stay free of responsibilities for the time being. He preferred the excitement of moving into the bed of any responsive woman at a moment's notice. He loved having no luggage to weigh him down. He carried no shaving kit, but went daily to the barber, and when his shirt and underwear became too foul, he would dump them and buy new. And only when he noticed a woman heave with the stench of him as he pressed her onto the bed, he asked to use the washbowl and soap as a farewell gesture.

Between the interludes with women, Bill hired a room at the Queen and Artichoke, a dingy pub down an alley by the railway. Up the dark little stairs at the side of the bar, in the tiny room, he flopped down on the iron bedstead and felt in charge of his own life. There was no one to question his next move, he was free. Someday he would have a permanent address. In the meantime, he enjoyed the lifestyle. It was exciting and full of possibilities.

Of late, the music hall had become his favourite haunt. He loved the lights and the warmth. He sat at his table, brown hat tipped at a saucy angle, feeling the trickle of liquor down his throat, smoking a cigar.

He found it easy to pick up women here, for he looked a prosperous fellow. He always insisted he went home to their place. This, they reasoned, was because his home was too grand for them, and Bill encouraged this idea.

❦

George and Charlotte were married in the tiny church on the estate at Easter. Charlotte wore a gown of wild silk with a long veil of Brussels lace used by many generations. She made her own bouquet of lilies of the valley and white moss roses.

Eliza felt she had never seen anything so beautiful and her eyes misted over with happiness. The only jarring note was the fear that Bill might turn up even though she had paid him well to stay away.

But she need not have worried. Bill was in love with his own way of life and did not want to put anything in the way of it.

Whenever he ran out of money, he would appear as the factory closed and, without a word, Eliza would give him a bag of gold sovereigns.

He was the dark shadow in her life. She believed he would be the reason for the end of her dream, for ever present in her mind was the belief that some great cataclysm would sweep away her run of good luck, end it for ever and push her back into the gutter.

But Charles was always there to reassure her. He had become very dear to her. She saw him frequently and when he went away for a while, she regularly received flowers from him.

Often they would spend happy evenings in her comfortable drawing room and Alice would serve them supper in front of the fire as they listened to music on the gramophone. Always as he said goodbye, Charles would take her in his arms and gently kiss her. Always her eyes would prick with tears.

'Whatever am I to think, Eliza, when my kisses bring tears to your eyes?'

'I'm just not used to it, Charles.'

'You are not used to tenderness, dear one.'

'No, I've never known it before . . . but . . .'

'Yes?'

'I'll tell you one thing. I like it.'

⚘

The war still raged. The battles of the Somme, of the Ancre and of Gallipoli took a terrible toll. The battle of Jutland, at sea plunged the country into a state of appalling darkness.

So it was that, in the face of all this horror, because of the demand for more uniforms, the factory flourished.

Since his marriage, George had grown stronger and more authoritative to a marked degree.

One night Eliza was in the office late. She had been to a dinner given by the Chamber of Commerce and was wearing a gown of midnight-blue satin, heavily embroidered down the panels. The low-cut neckline of the dress sat gracefully on the rounded contours of her shoulders. She made a perfect picture as she sat halfway between the shadows and the lamplight above. Before her on the desk was a pile of cloth samples. One by one she examined them in the light.

It was a stormy night. The heavy rain lashed against the windows. Somewhere, a door banged in the wind. Eliza hardly noticed. She knew Eli would see to it, he scarcely left the place. She could hear footsteps. Yes, Eli must be there. She continued to examine the samples. The footsteps

grew nearer, but they were not the sure and heavy tread
of Eli, but were uneven, as if the person were unsteady, or
drunk.

She sat as still as stone as the footsteps stumbled on the
stairs, then she became as cold as ice when the office door
burst open and Bill stood swaying there.

"Ello Liza. I've just come for a little talk.'

'I've nothing to say to you.'

'Oh no, lass, but I've got something to say to you
though. Plenty, in fact. I'll sit 'ere, because we may as
well be comfortable. We're in for a long night.' Bill pulled
up a chair and sat close to her at the desk. He leaned
across and reached for the sherry. 'How about a little
drink then, it's a heck of a night.'

She slapped his hand. 'From the smell of you, you've
had enough.'

'Nay Liza, don't be like that, and don't get shirty,
because by the time I've told you my story you'll agree to
anything, anything.'

It was warm in the office. Bill knew he held the trump
card and proceeded slowly to savour the moment. He
lifted his glass, peering over the rim at the picture she
made.

'By God, Liza, you've grown into a handsome woman.
I fancy a bit of that.' And he reached out to touch the
curve of her breast.

Snatching up a ruler from the desk, she cracked him sharply over the knuckles. 'Get on with it, or get out.'

Bill laughed. 'I'm enjoying this,' he said. 'Of late, Liza, you've been very good to me.'

'Not from choice.'

'No matter. These little handouts you're kind enough to give me have given me a better life. In fact, I'm having a very pleasant time. These days, I get around a lot, far more than I ever did. I mix with all sorts, sporting people, a very lively crowd. I follow the horses, I take an interest in the racing, I go to the meetings. Sometimes as far away as Doncaster.'

'Get on with it. What are you coming to?'

Ignoring her completely, Bill lit a cigar. 'As I was saying, the sporting world. Yes, then there is boxing, I follow that as well, I think nothing of going to Barnsley or even Manchester to see a boxer with a bit of style.'

'What is this to me?'

'Wait a minute, Liza, wait a minute. I'm getting to it. I also . . .' He pulled on his cigar. 'I also enjoy the theatrical life. Most nights I'm to be found in the music hall or variety theatre. It's a very nice class of person I meet there. Very pleasant. Very friendly.'

'Well, you're all right then, aren't you?'

'Just about, Liza. Just about. But then, you must notice in what I've been talking about, what I've been telling you, there's no mention of a home life, no mention of a family.'

'What are you getting at?'

'I've decided to seek a bit of background. Maybe settle down a bit. Perhaps I might buy a little house. Only a humble home but good enough for my grandchild.'

'Exactly what do you mean?'

'George's, I've heard she's having a bairn and I'll want to see him.'

'Never, never.'

'Oh yes, I think so, Liza. I think so this time. He's my son, my flesh and blood. You can't deny that. I'm a father he can be proud of. I'm very presentable.'

His good humour frightened her.

'I'm going back a bit now.' He gave a dramatic pause. 'Not that long after I'd set up wi' Ada, things weren't going too well. She was expecting this bairn and she were a right misery. Sick all the time and always moaning. She needed this and she needed that, always wanting money. Well, I was a bit pushed for cash at the time, not much work about you know, so I wasn't pickin' up much.

'Now, it so happened that I needed to go back to the house for a few tools I'd left in the cellar, and, of course, while I was there I had a little look about for the odd shillin' you might have put in the pot. I remembered you sometimes shoved a bit in the floorboards under the bed.'

Eliza froze. 'You knew about that?'

'Course I did. Don't be daft. Always checked up on yer. But, I must say, I never 'ad such a funny find as I did that day. The remains of a corset, Liza. Aye, it'd been handsome but now it were shredded.

'What a funny thing to save, I thought. Must have cost a lot at one time. Some woman must have passed it on where you were scrubbin', but why save the bits? I couldn't make it out so I put the floorboard back and you left that place soon after.

'I thought no more about it. Until now.'

He drew his chair closer towards her and laughed wheezily into her face.

He then pressed a large, stinking, slobbering kiss over her mouth. He grabbed her shoulders and held her still. 'I'll have thee yet, Liza,' he whispered hoarsely.

She tried to raise the ruler again but he held her wrists and growled into her face with a voice dark with emotion.

'Nar, listen.' He sat back in his chair and pulled on his cigar knowing she was his prisoner. 'Going as I do to the music hall, to the theatre, I meet a good class of girl there. Very nice lasses, very friendly. Sometimes, they let me stay with them as they know I haven't got a home to go to.' He paused for a moment. 'Aye, nice lasses. But there were this one that really took my eye. She looked proper fetching and it was said she liked a bit of this and a bit of that. And you'll know what I mean, Liza, now you're a woman of the world.'

His eyes narrowed as he sped the arrow home. He spoke slowly, his voice low.

'Well, last week, I spent a few days in her company. In fact, I spent a few days and nights in her bed. She's good company, chatters a lot. She enjoys her customers. She likes their little fancies. How different they all are. One wants a bit of this, another wants a bit of that, and she's not against talking about it.

'She told me all sorts of things that made me laugh and some I'd never heard of before. And then she told me about this chap that used to visit her a few years ago. A big fat man, gingerish hair, lots of freckles. All he wanted was to be tied up and smacked. He died about that time and it turned out that he was the mayor.

'He died in Alderman Helliwell's house, on the night you left, Liza. And do you know what she told me, Liza? That he wore a corset to hold in his great big belly. She could remember them clear as day, because they were so fancy for a man, black satin, wi' little rosebuds.

'The other thing was that he would never let them out of his sight for he said he had a fortune hidden in them seams. And do you know, Liza, all of a sudden it came to me. That day, when I went back to our house and lifted the floorboard, and there was this heap of corset, I put two and two together, Liza, and I made a lot more than four.'

She looked at him like a rabbit frozen by a snake. This was it. All was ended for her. But the worst of it was that George would be dealt this blow at the height of his happiness. She sat before him, speechless and vulnerable.

He knew he had her in his power and it inflamed all his senses. He wanted her more at that moment than he had wanted anything in his life. He threw himself over her and throbbing with drink and ecstasy he whispered, 'Liza, come on, lass, set up house wi' me. Let's enjoy the spoils together, then you silence me for ever.' His hands slithered down her body. Dragged her hair from its comb.

She sprang to life. 'Get off, you foul rotten bugger,' she cried. But his fingers tightened around her. She pushed him in desperation but he was a very strong man in his excited state. She picked up the ruler and cracked it over his head, but he scarcely felt it.

She reached desperately for the iron window pole, lifted it high and brought it crashing down upon his shoulders as he knelt clasping her legs.

With a scream of pain, he leaped backwards. 'Bitch, bitch,' he snarled at her and walked backwards, shielding his face with his hands against the blows she was raining on him. But by now she could not stop.

'Stop it, Liza, stop!' Bill cried as he backed away from her, but she followed him relentlessly beating him in her passion.

'Down you go,' she cried. 'Get down them stairs and out, go on, get down there.'

He kept on backing away to reach the stairs. Suddenly, he saw her raise the pole again. Expecting a heavy blow, he flung himself against the railings with such a force that a weak joint was broken, and, arms across his face, he went crashing down to the floor of the factory below.

Eliza stood for one moment, petrified, then dropping the pole she went forward, leaned over the rail and saw Bill lying splayed out, very still on the floor below.

She went to examine him and could see that he was dead. A small trickle of blood crept from his nostrils. She moved quickly to wipe it away in case it stained the floor. He had to be moved before he left any evidence.

Quickly, she pulled towards her the overhead crane used for moving bundles of cloth, and slipping the hook under his belt, she hauled him high into the air. There he hung like a giant spider, his broken neck giving a curious twist to his head.

Eliza worked the crane to carry him down the length of the factory floor to the end of the building. He floated strangely through the air, drifting slightly from side to side, as if at any moment he would leap down and threaten her.

She looked up at him and suddenly felt helpless, not knowing what to do now. Surely this was the end for her. Nothing could overcome this. But as she stood there in blank despair, a shadow appeared in the doorway. It was Eli.

Without a word Eli stepped forward and lowered the body to the ground. Then he turned to her and said, 'I'll see to this, missus, you look round for owt he's left here. I can see his hat over yonder, his stick there, give 'em to me.' And with that he picked up the dead man and slung him over his shoulder.

As he walked towards the door to the cellars, Eli slowly turned to her. 'Go home now,' he said. 'Go home and have a good lot of brandy before you go to bed; we'll speak in the morning.'

And then he was gone and so was Bill, leaving no evidence that he had ever been there.

Chapter 7

After a sleepless night, Eliza arrived early at the factory. She found Eli in a small storeroom outside the main building.

She did not need to ask.

'Sit down, missus,' he said. 'I'll tell you what you want to know. He's well put away under a cellar on the lower floor. Happen you don't know this, but underneath the cellars, there's steps down to another floor, very dark, nobody goes there, very wet it is down there, he'll rot quick he will.'

'Eli, oh Eli . . .' Eliza began to stammer.

'Enough, missus. It's sealed, it's done, it's finished.'

'But what if they come looking for him?'

'Who will look for him, missus? Nobody. He'll never be missed, he weren't anywhere for more than five minutes at a time, he had no roots. He were a waster.'

'But he was a man.'

'He was not a man. He was a rat, and I think no more of it than if I killed a rat. That's what you do with vermin, you get rid of them.'

'I still don't know.'

'Missus, when I went through that war in Africa I had men killed all around me. Good men, aye, and good pals of mine. They had all their lives in front of them, and I saw them blown to pieces and die screaming. They were the ones should have lived. Think nothing of it, missus. It never happened.'

Eliza, still trembling, went up to her office and had some sherry. She noted even the broken rails were mended, so nothing showed. Dear Eli, what a friend he was. She had never heard him say so many words at one time.

❦

'Is anything the matter, Mam?' said George after a few weeks. 'You don't look too well. Maybe you should take a holiday.'

He was worried about her. One day he had found her down in the cellars, trying to open an old door.

'Whatever are you doing? You don't want to go down there, it's only another lot of cellars, it's awful, it's wet and full of rats.'

'I wanted to see it. I've never been down there.'

'You never want to.'

'Yes, I do. Take me far enough down for me to see what it's like.'

He did. And supported by him, she leaned over the rotting balustrade to look on Bill's grave.

The stench was sickening, pools of water stood on the filthy floors, rats ran into gaping holes and wetness trickled down the crumbling walls.

'It's hopeless,' said George. 'It's too far gone to do anything with it. It should be filled in.'

George was even more concerned about his mother when he was told she had been sleepwalking, as she had never done this before. He would have taken her away himself but could not leave Charlotte during her pregnancy.

It was finally decided that Eliza should go to Richmond in Surrey, for a complete change of scene. A caring hotel with a nurse in charge was found, high on a hill, with a winding river glittering below. She would be there for some weeks.

⁂

One evening shortly before Christmas, having a slight cold which made her feel sleepy, Eliza had a hot milk with a good stir of honey and brandy and retired early to bed.

She felt restless at first, haunted by thoughts of things past, but eventually fell into a deep sleep. So deep, that when she was shaken awake by Alice it was difficult to gather her senses.

'Wake up, Mrs Northrop, wake up,' said Alice. There was urgency in her voice. She rubbed Eliza's hands. 'Come on, madam, come to.'

Eliza in a daze could just see the outline of Alice's face bent above her in the darkness. 'What's the time? It's still dark.'

'It's three o'clock in the morning. You've got to wake up. Here, put this on, or you'll catch your death.' She dragged the warm dressing gown over her mistress. 'Now, come to the window.'

Eliza went sleepily to the window and what she saw when Alice drew the curtain made her spring wide awake.

It was a night of fitful black clouds and faint moonshine. The countryside was bathed in wintry darkness. Alice pointed. There, high in the sky, slowly entering and re-entering the black clouds was an object like a long silver cigar. It gave just a slight hum as it moved menacingly over the moors towards the town.

It was a Zeppelin making its way with a deadly load.

Streaks of light followed by huge explosions lit up the night sky over the town, where the Zeppelin slid past like an evil snake and disappeared into the dark night.

The town woke up immediately.

Ben came running up the stairs shouting, 'They've hit

the mills. They've hit the mills. Come on, missus, I've got the trap, we must go yonder.'

Eliza did not want to waste time dressing, but Alice made her put on warm clothes and a fur coat. 'For the sake of five minutes, missus. You've got a cold already. You'll not be wanting pneumonia.'

'Hurry then, hurry,' snapped Eliza as she dragged the clothes on with trembling fingers.

She sat beside Ben in the trap as they went out through the gates and joined the ever-growing crowd of people moving towards the disaster.

The flames had now taken over. Great buildings stood outlined against the sky in a sheet of light and smoke. Every yard they went, their progress was slowed by people crowding onto the streets. Clad in a strange mixture of attire they came shouting, anxiously wondering where the fire would spread. The little trap stood immobile in the swirl of humanity.

In the glow of the light it looked like the day of judgement to Eliza. *Her* day of judgement. If that blazing mill was hers, all the foundations would be exposed, and when the stones cooled they would find a skeleton with a pocket watch, rings, money in its pocket and a broken neck.

Her downfall was near.

They never got to the scene that night, so hemmed in

LIZ SMITH

were they by the crowds. Eventually they were turned
back by police fearing for people's lives in the crush.

Eliza went to her room. Sitting in her great chair by the
fire, she waited for the news that would bring her doom.

Two mills near Eliza's were completely gutted and had
to be demolished. Her mill was touched, causing one
wall to collapse. Some storerooms and all the cellars were
filled with rubble. As the cellars were in a bad state it
was considered best to fill them in, so they could become
the foundation for the replacement building. Bill's body
would not be found and Eliza felt released. She sent a
large donation to the children's hospital and to the home
for stray animals.

❧

The week after Christmas, a barman from the Queen and
Artichoke identified a man taken from the river as Bill
Northrop. It was very difficult to tell; he had been in the
water a long time and his clothes were eaten away. But
the barman thought he recognized his boots.

Early in the spring, Charlotte gave birth to her one and
only child, a son named James.

Afraid that something would go wrong, Eliza could
hardly bring herself to see him. Surely, with all her sins she
could not have a perfect grandchild. But quite the opposite.

George called for her in his motor car one day soon

after the birth, and took her to the nursing home. When Eliza peered into the crib her heart stopped with joy, then burst into excited beating like the loud clamour of bells and a thousand butterflies bursting upwards into the sky.

She looked down into his new-born face and fell in love as she had never done before. She knew she had found the centre of her life. The point of her universe. The object of her love until the day she died.

She cried with happiness. But James was surrounded by people who felt exactly the same. Charlotte looked on him with amazement that she should ever have a child. George was filled with a golden glow and had to pinch himself to believe in his happiness. Charles and Lydia were as loving as delighted grandparents.

With such an event in her life, Eliza began to feel more like her old self, and visited the baby nearly every day.

But sadness was not far away, when in early summer, Ruby Birtle died of the TB that had developed in her dreadful asylum.

Eliza was filled with sorrow. That bright star. That joyful little soul, born to do so much and extinguished like a candle simply because she had a child. Eliza remembered her laughter and mourned her because she was not meant for that end.

Chapter 8

With the Armistice in 1918, George and Charlotte began to develop the estates into commercial flower gardens. This gave work to a few of the many servicemen returning shattered from the war. Meanwhile, parts of the mill were leased out to a firm making fashion wear.

George's interest in manufacturing began to fade with the demand now the war was over. He did not see the point of saving the business for James. Who knew what future lay ahead for that little boy? He concentrated instead more on large glass houses to grow all kinds of vegetables and flowers.

It was good work for men fighting the effects of mustard gas, of terrible wounds that left body and soul weak and eyes sightless. It was good work for men haunted by the horror of the trenches.

Each change in the process meant more workers, advertising just a few jobs brought so many applicants flooding in, for these were sorry times. Interviews were held at the factory, the gardens being a little out of town.

Jottings

Walking down the corridor where the hopefuls were gathered made George's heart bleed. The sad people sat silent on the benches, thin clothes neatly mended and patched, eyes downcast. George wished he could choose them all.

❦

Charles's wife Lydia knew about Eliza but could not hate her. She admired her qualities and could understand why Charles sought her company.

Had his interest been directed towards a dazzling society beauty in the world that Lydia knew so well and was now deprived of, she would have been painfully jealous. But how could she resent his friendship, even love, of this woman? Lydia had to admit she actually liked Eliza herself. Life had been so tough on her that her character had emerged strong as steel.

Besides, his caring for Eliza had not altered Charles's feelings for Lydia one jot. He still came rushing to her room on his return, where, as usual, they would have supper together and laugh and talk over the day's events, even if they included Eliza.

With the coming of James, Eliza became an occasional visitor to take tea with Lydia, and to share their love of the little boy.

Lydia knew how precious her days were with James.

Eliya
1920

How soon the time would fly and the tiny boy would be gone. How school would take him away from her. How she would become smaller in his ever-growing world. She dreaded the time when he was big enough to go away to school, maybe grudgingly only giving her a little time in the holidays.

But before that day came, one morning on her beautiful bed, Lydia did not wake.

Eliza and Charles mourned together for her. Often on their walks they would visit her grave and shed tears for her frustrated life.

Soon the main preoccupation of Eliza's life became her beloved Jamie. Her golden boy with his good humour, his laughter, and love of all things beautiful, particularly music.

From the age of seven he had taken to the violin, and it was obvious from the beginning that music was his future.

Like Lydia, Eliza felt jealous of his school widening his life, his friends taking him away from her. But it was inevitable and she had to accept it.

Visiting him at school on open days, as she sat on the great lawns with Charles, George and Charlotte, she could only marvel at the scene. The majestic buildings of the great public school, the flutter of dresses, cricket whites, parasols and teacups. The laughter, the discreet conversation, the well-being of it all made her remember the little penny school in the back streets of Clecklewyke she had attended as a child. Even that building had now been demolished and the impatient teacher showing them how to write on their squeaky little slates was long gone.

One day during the summer holidays, James, as he always did, walked into her drawing room through the French windows. The sun touched his golden hair and skin, and added a twinkle to his blue-grey eyes.

After ecstatic greetings they talked about his future, where he would study music. The world was open to him.

'Gran,' said James. 'I have a shock for you. I'm changing course. I have decided to do medicine.'

'But your music?'

'I can do that as well, Gran. I can use music in my medicine. Why does healing always have to be so gloomy? Why can't I add music, or painting, or dance to a bottle of physic?'

'I'm sure nobody's thought of that one.'

'Oh Gran, I long to do something to make the world a bit better, a bit happier. There's so much greyness. Why must everything be grim? I'm sure people would recover more easily in bright surroundings.'

'I know what you mean, love. I know our hospital well.'

And memories flooded over Eliza of the long dark wards and the grim matron, of Ruby. The thought of that little lost star made her eyes prick with tears.

With the years, the rheumatic pain had returned to Eliza's legs. She took to using a stick but was still able to get about though more slowly these days. It was at night her legs troubled her and she was easier sitting in her great armchair by the fire. Here she often slept by night and dozed by day.

She still shared her thoughts with Charles, although the years had slowed down their travels and the war in Europe had stopped their trips to the continent.

George and Charlotte were very busy growing vegetables for the latest war effort and James was in Ireland working hard with his finals to become a doctor.

Early in March 1941, Eliza felt restless and irritable one day. She needed to get out of the house. Putting on her fur coat she made her way round the paths, her two cats following her and scampering around her feet.

The grass was white with hoar frost. A spider's web, touched with diamonds, hung between the branches of a tree, and a robin sang.

Eliza smiled. It was a good omen. Robins were lucky.

The air froze her breath and her fingers began to chill. She should go in.

She stood on the path and surveyed her little kingdom. It felt strangely detached and silent in the freezing cold. The darkening sky made the silver ground shine and the outlines of the bare trees were as a drawing in charcoal on opalescent paper.

The robin hopped on a twig, quite near, and the young maid called her in to say that tea was ready. It was laid on a silver tray in front of a roaring log fire. Eliza felt so relaxed in its warmth that she soon fell asleep in the chair.

Suddenly she was awakened by a sharp sound. Someone was rattling her French windows. She could scarcely see, for the light was nearly gone, but James's voice reassured her and she crossed the room to unlock the door.

She returned to her chair to switch on the lamp, and when she turned, she saw James standing before her in a sailor's uniform. Her heart froze.

He took her hands and kissed her. 'I had to do it, Gran, I could not stay out in times like these.'

'Your finals?'

'They can wait. It will soon be over. I may be away for a while so I have forty-eight hours' leave. I can't stay, haven't even told Mother and Father yet. I may need a lot of time for that.'

He turned by the windows and, putting on his cap, gave her a salute, then hurried quickly through the garden.

Eliza sat as if turned to stone. Outside, snow softly

drifted. She knew the moment had come. Here was her payment to be made, the most cruel blow of all. Any one of the earlier threats would have been kinder than this. When James had put his cap on, it was written in golden thread around the ribbon: HMS HOOD.

HMS *Hood* was sunk with all hands on 24 May 1941.

That day the maid brought the newspapers to her mistress sleeping in her chair, but could not rouse her.

Hello

I've always been a bit psychic.
At least, they used to say so.
I can't exactly remember who they were.
But I can remember what they said.
Not everything,
you understand.
But I can remember the words.
Now that's funny.
I know that words are called words.
And I know which words are used to call different things.
Without thinking.
Instinctively.
For instance,
I can tell you where I live.
I live in the shadow of a great rock shelf,
where the water is dark and cool.
There are some weedy things,
like white grasses,

for me to eat.
I can eat without moving.
Without going anywhere.
Just like the stuff I grew in my garden . . .
There you go.
I came out with it,
without thinking,
without batting an eyelid.
And yet,
in this state,
I have never seen a garden.
Not that I had much of one then.
Some people did.
Some people had big gardens.
Big.
Like the countryside.
They had dogs.
I can remember the dogs as if it were yesterday.
But it wasn't yesterday.
Yet,
in a way,
I suppose it was.
Right off the top of my scales,
I'd say it was a couple of million years ago.
It all passed in a flash.
I lived in a big block of homes stuck together,

made of red brick.

They were called flats.

Mine had a little balcony.

Just big enough for me to sit in a chair

and grow a few tomatoes in a bag.

I was either a man or a woman.

I don't know which.

It doesn't matter.

They were all men or women,

and there were lots of them.

I call them the woes.

The streets were full of them.

Everything was full of them.

Trains.

Buses.

Shops.

There were always too many in front of me.

Getting in my way wherever I went.

And it wasn't just the place where I lived.

It was the same everywhere.

Some parts of the world were even more crowded than others.

And, to make matters worse,

they used different words.

So they could understand each other.

It must have been all right in the beginning.

In the beginning there were not many woes.
But they multiplied so quickly
that, by the time I arrived in the world,
which was at the very end of the woes' time on earth,
it was awful.
Just a fight to survive.
You were lucky if you found a bit of space and food.
Millions couldn't find enough food.
So they died.
At the same time,
other millions wasted food
in the most extravagant manner.
They were a weird lot,
the woes.
They started to fight.
I suppose
to start with
they just got in each other's way,
and gave each other a little push.
Then they started to throw stones.
They were a very progressive lot.
They quickly went on to better ideas for chopping each
other into little bits.
I smile
when I think of them all dressed up in tinny stuff,
just to throw stones.

If they fell over they couldn't get up.

They sat on horses to make themselves look important.

They were very good at killing each other.

Some of the woes spent whole lifetimes inventing things

that would kill more and more in one go.

In the end

they could kill millions

just by pressing a button.

You could tell how bright they were.

They were always wanting to test these machines

to make sure they could really make a mess.

The bigger the better,

they said.

And they were always carting off their secret machines

to pretty little islands.

Or remote deserts.

Some woes marched up and down with home-made banners,

saying, 'No. No. No.'

But it made no difference at all.

I hardly noticed what was going on.

Because it was happening all the time

and I had my living to earn.

All the time I was on earth

I was being told to sacrifice.

Suffer.

And endure.
Then things would get better.
They didn't.
But the night the brick fell I knew something had changed.
I was sitting on my balcony,
next to my bag of tomato compost,
when,
for no reason,
this brick fell.
From the flat above.
I watched it settle on my wall
and I looked at it.
As I looked
a strange swirling mist enveloped me
and clouded my senses.
I struggled to look through it.
When it cleared
I was still looking at the brick.
But I was lost in it.
The whole universe stretched out before me.
Only seen behind the screen of the composition of the brick.
I saw every particle of the brick in great and shining light.
Each particle was big and rounded.
And gathered together in groups of different pale colours.
Here and there were gaps which turned into vast openings.

Dark passageways
leading off into infinity.
I felt I could swim down them.
It was a sensuous feeling.
I left my body
and floated.
As one with the universe.
I knew I was nothing.
I was not as important as the brick,
whose atoms continued to glow and move
in their patterns
around each other.
Some of them
moved towards me and burst into light.
I was just settling down into my new state.
I didn't want to bother being me.
Ever again.
The time had not arrived for me to stay.
The mist swirled round me again,
and I was in my chair.
And the brick was a brick,
was a brick.
But things were never the same again.
And I knew I was living in an altered state.
I carried on.
I went to my job every day in the launderette.

It all became a dream.
I talked to people,
but didn't really hear what they were saying.
Washing came.
Washing went.
I did things automatically.
It was possible to live my kind of life not fully switched
on.
So that when something real happened.
like the brick.
Well, it was so loud and shining,
everything else seemed colourless.
I didn't like the next flash of reality.
Not at all.
I was terrified.
I was helping a person through the door with her trolley.
She was very fat
and her trolley was loaded with washing.
She was pushing the trolley.
I was pulling it.
When
it happened again.
The swirling mist.
I turned my head to look at the car showroom over the
road.
And saw infinity.

But it was dark.

It was evil.

The stench was horrible.

The huge, moving particles seemed to compose some sort of

gigantic head,

drifting together like a rotting corpse.

The side of the street where the road should have gone up to the park was completely filled with a prehistoric creature of such vastness, there was no sky.

Behind it stood another, and another, and another.

Each one composed of hideous particles, drifting in and out of each other.

Moving,

and slipping,

and slithering.

'Don't take me,'

I tried to shout.

'Don't take me.'

I was still shouting when the mist swirled away.

I found myself with my head pressed into the enormous tits of the fat woe.

I could smell the sweat and grease of her dirty skin.

It was a wonderful, comforting experience.

I clung to her,

babbling like an idiot.

The manager and two customers eventually managed
to unclench my fingers from her jumper.
'Take a holiday,'
said the manager.
I didn't go anywhere.
I knew something important was about to happen,
and evil unleashed.
I crouched in the shadow of my room.
Or on my little balcony.
I carried my little radio and a good supply of batteries.
I listened to voices incessantly.
I couldn't bear not to.
Call-in programmes.
Medical problems.
Symptoms in sickening details.
New plays.
New films.
Always, always, quiz games.
Every hour.
The news.
I drifted in and out of sleep,
watched the days pass on the busy street beyond the
buildings.
News.
Some king had died.
Unemployment was up again.

There was an argument about a test in a desert.
Night fell.
I ate a tomato from my compost bag.
I had a stale roll and a piece of cheese.
I dozed.
The next news woke me.
A pop singer was getting married again.
They were going ahead with the test in the desert.
I made myself a cup of tea,
watched the lights come on in the streets and the buses.
The guard at Woolworths began to lock the doors.
There was a sudden burst of cold rain
and people hurried home.
I stayed on my balcony.
I turned up my jacket collar
and wished I'd been to the betting shop.
It left me with nothing to hear on the racing results.
I poked around a bit in the kitchen cupboards.
Nothing much.
A half-eaten Chinese takeaway
and a small tin of beans.
The cat came in from next door.
I put the bean juice on a saucer for the cat.
I think I ate the beans.
Then I must have had a long sleep.
It was daylight in some floating time.

I took the last bit of money out of the electricity bill jar
and decided to go to Woolworths.
If I kept to the front of the shop I could still see my
balcony.
I would not take my eyes off it for a second.
I shuddered in my anxiety to get down the cement stairs.
Falling and slipping over the plastic rubbish bags
and tin cans.
I looked up.
It was still there.
My balcony.
I didn't know how I crossed the road,
but there I was.
At the food counter,
with my eyes fixed across the traffic.
Without looking down
I grabbed stuff.
I grabbed a newspaper from a litter bin.
When I looked up
the little cat was making her way along my balcony wall.
I felt a huge surge of relief.
The cat must be real.
I felt almost normal.
I seemed to have bought some condensed milk,
so we shared that.
I had some mushy peas.

Then I had a look at the newspaper.

There was a whole page of comments by important people.

They were not equally happy about the test.

But all agreed

it just had to be.

There were so many questions to be answered.

They just needed one more test.

It would be the final one.

It was.

I searched the paper,

but found nothing about anyone having experiences such as mine.

And I was so ordinary.

I had never done a thing.

I liked being at the launderette,

because it was handy for the betting shop and takeaway.

But if that job packed up there'd be another.

It always had to be somewhere near because of my flat.

Or I could go on social security.

I didn't mind.

I liked watching the woes in the street.

And the big red buses.

And all the funny names on the front.

I thought it strange that all the revelations happened to me.

It should have been to the Archbishop of Canterbury.
Or the Queen.
Or the Prime Minister.
They would have known what to do.
Which pigeon hole to pop it into.
Which publicity firm to use.
The cat sat on my lap.
A daisy had grown in the compost bag.
The news came on my little radio at regular intervals.
There was an outbreak of multiple births in America.
A reporter named Jim was calling from the scene of the test.
The line was very crackly
and it was a long way away.
Jim said it had all gone to plan.
The generals were very pleased.
Protestors in a nearby town had been arrested.
The results of this test would be of enormous value
to the human race.
It was quite dark when I woke again.
Not many people in the street.
It was drizzly.
Then Jim came on again.
Crackle. Crackle.
Telegrams were pouring in,
he said.
From all the heads of government.

Congratulating the generals
on the success of the test.
The hole in the desert,
said Jim,
was the biggest ever created,
and every leader was satisfied.
The generals were more than happy.
It all went quiet for a few days.
An envelope was pushed under my door.
It was from the launderette.
Fifty pounds wages
and a note saying don't come back until I was really well.
I had been listening to a play on the radio.
Watching the red buses in the street
filling and emptying.
When there was a news flash.
It was Jim.
He said
the generals had been called to the test site
and further news would be given as soon as it came in.
The programmes went on.
The next news was normal.
Same as ever.
It wasn't until the next afternoon that Jim came on again.
Even through the crackle I could hear the concern in
his voice.

The hole in the desert was still growing.
The sand was still trickling in.
There was to be a report from the watch every half hour.
A programme on inflation was interrupted by another
news flash.
Jim again.
The generals had reassembled
and the lookout was to report every twenty minutes.
A soldier had stopped mid-sentence.
Sand was trickling in at a faster rate.
Once I woke to find the cat,
back arched,
hair spread into a wide brush,
eyes so wide that I started to float in them.
But I wasn't surprised now,
and I clung onto her eyelid as hard as I could.
I clambered out and lay in the strange area
where the hair turns direction
between the corner of the eye and the ear.
I was nearly blinded by the glorious yellow
of the atoms in her eyes.
Bathed in golden light.
What a clever little creature she was.
She could feel it coming.
Far ahead of all the people in the street.
Far ahead of the Chief of Police.

Or the Pope.

Or Mr Brindsley at the off-licence,

who is a know-all.

Jim's reports became more and more frantic.

His disappearance was reported in the *Evening Standard*.

The ever-quickening sand had spread too quickly over his base.

After that

so many lines of communication disappeared.

There was no word from the whole of the American continent.

There was a brief period from Canada.

A peep from a remote station in Alaska.

Then silence.

Russia seemed to go very quickly.

The Middle East had so much sand anyway,

it went like an egg timer.

When it started on Eastern Europe

the little cat got very upset.

I cut up a sleeping tablet into her food.

Down in the street

the barricades went up.

Police stood by.

Troops rolled up in great tanks.

The people were sealed in.

They continued to shop for whatever was left.

They bought everything they could find.
Anything.
With the population in the grip of the military,
plans were made to get the VIPs to safety.
Innocent-looking hillsides proved to be cities
of underground hideaways.
A great lid was lowered over the Barbican.
It proved to be a deep shelter for many souls,
true to its original design.
It all went according to plan.
It took quite a long time for them to realize
what they had done.
By then
it was too late.
All the Members of Parliament were together
in their steel shelter
when they were sucked to the centre of the earth.
Plans had to be quickly altered for what was left
of government
and captains of industry.
All the roads around the airport were closed.
Planes were taking off.
One every minute.
To fly . . .
To fly . . .
Where?

To land . . .

Nowhere.

They had forgotten to take this into account.

The planes could only fly until the fuel ran out.

They had nowhere to land.

When it was close

I gave the cat a meal

with a tablet,

and settled on the balcony with her asleep on my knee.

I watched the great trickle move silently down the high street.

Suddenly,

all was quiet.

Very quiet.

The shops.

The offices.

Just folded over.

Woolworths went like a ballet dancer taking a bow.

Buses looked like great streaks of red paint being drawn downwards.

The waving arms of the passengers making a thrilling design.

What should I have done with my knowledge of infinity?

Should I have gone to the church?

Which church?

Which organized belief

could have coped with the vastness of it?
When it reached me
I turned over softly
with the cat on my lap.
I just whispered,
'I know there is evil,
let me go to the light.'
And I did go to the light.
Every atom was huge and beautiful.
Palest colours
shining.
Like the first time.
Things vaguely kept their shape.
Woolworths was just ahead of me.
A little further on.
St Paul's drifted gently down.
As fast as the seas were thrown into the centre,
they were thrown out as hissing steam.
For me
the light got brighter
and then took me into itself.
The pressure of the steam jets
threw the ball that had been the earth
violently around.
It was pushed.
Hard and dark as a cricket ball

into alien spheres.
For millennia it floated in darkness
and fearsome gases.
Through endless channels of infinite stars.
Through fire
and consuming heat.
Until
many millions of years later,
as we counted them
but during which they did not exist at all,
a disturbance
in a distant atmosphere
pushed the hard,
brownish-coloured ball
into a benign stream.
It was raining only softly now.
And the hard surface relaxed a little.
In the vast aeons of time.
Measureless.
Floating.
One day
I just opened my eyes,
and here I was.
In this rock pool.
I was very happy in this deep shadow.
Then

HELLo.

I noticed a patch of light ahead.

Eventually,

I moved into it.

And,

do you know,

it was warm.

Such a pleasant sensation.

I started to do it all the time.

And then

one day

I noticed a slope upwards.

Carefully

I crawled up to it.

Always keeping my eyes on my shadowed home.

My scales erect with fear.

The warmth was there too,

I could even breathe.

It felt good.

The light came at regular intervals.

I got used to it.

I began to enjoy being out here.

I have found some greenish grass to eat.

Rather like the whitish grass in the pool.

I can eat without moving.

I like it.

I have decided to stay here.

The Pea-green Suit

Kevin was pleased he had chosen pea green for his linen suit.

Noel, the hairdresser at Chez Noel, had chosen bright pink for *his* linen suit and had worn it on his celebrity hair day. Kevin had seen him when he had passed the salon on his way to work at the town hall.

If I ever have a celebrity day, vowed Kevin to himself, I'll wear a linen suit.

And now he had both, a celebrity day and a linen suit.

Kevin had always wanted to be famous. Best of all, a famous writer. He wanted people to nudge each other in the supermarket and whisper, 'That's Kevin Brown, the famous writer – must be worth a fortune, yet he still comes round the shops like us.'

Yes, one day he would astonish them, they would lean against their bicycles and watch him pass.

That was why he had invested £65 of his Post Office savings in the so-easy writing course. They had liked his

Kevin always wanted to be famous.

work. Always put a kind word and a star on his stories. There was even a half promise he might be included in the paperback they published yearly at the pupils' expense.

He had heard nothing now for some time except a reminder that, if he wanted to be included in next year's course he must pay a deposit now – oh yes, and the fee had gone up to £72.50 because of rising costs.

❧

Then suddenly, out of the blue it came. An invitation to a literary reception at the Plaza, organized by the culture department at the town hall in cooperation with the Voda publishing company, to launch the latest book of the very famous novelist, Miss Ivy O'Grady.

Ticket to Heaven was supposed to be more daring and sexually explicit than any of her twenty-four previous novels. It was a great triumph for the culture department to have her come along in person, and they were all getting their best suits out of mothballs.

Although he passed it every day, Kevin had never been inside the Plaza. On his way to his grey little office he could observe the great marble hall, the polished brass, the dramatic lighting, and the front desk where very superior ladies questioned you as you entered. You would have to feel pretty good, thought Kevin, even to walk up to that desk.

That was what the pea-green linen suit would do. It would separate him from his daily life.

Kitty looked up from her cornflakes and spilled a large spoonful of milk down her flannelette nightie. She twisted her head round in disbelief. The spoon froze in the air as the milk grew cold on her breast.

'Blimey,' she said. Then could think of nothing better to say, so she said it again. 'Blimey.'

'I knew you'd like it, Ma,' said Kevin, and he patted her crocheted night cap back into place. 'It's for tomorrow.'

'Oh yeah. D'you want cornflakes or Sugar Puffs?'

Amazingly, tomorrow did come.

The pea-green suit lay draped over the exercise bicycle, so that it was the first thing Kevin saw when he opened his eyes.

He washed his armpits and squirted a lot of that spray that makes girls run after you in the street. He knew that was true because he'd seen it on the telly. Kevin was very sensitive to odour.

Kevin stood on the pavement in his linen suit and looked up at the building which seemed to pierce the sky. Once inside he noticed a board by the lift, announcing in gold letters: 'Literary Reception, Floor 16'.

Floor 16. Oh my God. He hated heights. Couldn't stand them. But at least if he crept into the lift, he wouldn't have to face the ladies behind the desk.

The lift arrived. He stepped in and stood there as casually as if he did it every day. The doors started to close, but they were thrust back by a strong red arm. A cleaner moved in beside him, dragging a huge plastic wheelie bucket with an assortment of mops and brushes clipped to the handrail. The woman was short and fat, her vast bosom draped in wine-coloured fabric with 'Plaza' printed across the front.

Kevin pressed number sixteen, and looked enquiringly at the cleaner.

'Twenty one for me,' she growled and took out a cigarette.

The lift shot up to the fifth floor, then stopped with a sickening jolt. Kevin's heart missed a beat. He looked fearfully at the woman who smoked impassively.

'Don't worry mate,' she said coolly. 'These lifts are always sticking. Bleedin' dangerous they are. Shoddy workmanship, an' all that bleeding brass and marble down there in the 'all.'

'I feel sick,' said Kevin.

'Lean on me mop,' she said.

Clutching on to the mop, he retched into the plastic container.

'Won't be long. Usually about five minutes.'

It was seven minutes, and to Kevin it seemed like seven hours. Just when he felt he must lie down on the floor, with a sudden jerk, the lift started.

On the sixteenth floor he had to rest against the wall for a minute before he faced the reception room. Feeling slightly dizzy, he braced himself to encounter the noisy throng.

Ivy O'Grady was a big woman who wore big jewellery. She had to, as anything delicate would look silly on that well-rounded form. Amber was her choice. Large lumps of it around her arms and ears. And her well-displayed breasts.

The colour of the amber clashed with the dark red, skin-tight dress she wore, but Ivy was defiant about colour; she believed in the more the better. To prove it, her hair was dyed a violent shade of carrot red, and her lipstick would have looked good on a pillar box.

Ivy was busy doing her act as the genteel, oh-so-famous novelist. With a smile fixed upon her vivid lips, it made her cheeks ache. Inside, she was seething with anger. What the hell was Ben, her publisher, doing sending her to a hole like this? She didn't need it. She just didn't need it. Hadn't she done book signings in all the great hotels of the world where people were civilized and sophisticated, where they knew how to dress and how to behave?

Not like this lot. Uncomfortable in their best suits and smelling of body perfumes.

Bit of everything here, all mixed in with sweat, thought Ivy. For Ivy had a sensitive nose.

She had protested to Ben in his impressive pannelled office, when he had suggested this town.

'You need to woo the semi-literates, my dear.' Ben spread his fingers and bit into his bagel. 'They're the ones who buy all the paperbacks, and your sales have been going down on the last three books.' He breathed into his handkerchief and wiped the grease off his fountain pen.

The humiliation. To have to stand smiling, in the middle of this crowd. And the damned thing had only just started. It would be going on for hours yet.

Her eyes, still smiling, sought desperately around the room. There was no way out. She was hemmed in by the sycophantic faces who mouthed their pointless inanities like goldfish. Then, suddenly, she noticed by the door a young man in a pea-green linen suit. He looked lost, bewildered and unsure of himself.

Ivy found this most endearing and decided he must be a long-lost friend. ''Scuse, 'scuse, there's my friend.' She broke loose from her tormentors and with arms raised, made a wild dive for the pea-green suit.

Kevin, still dazed from his incident in the lift, saw the bombshell separate from the crowd by the window and lunge straight towards him.

Miss Joy O'Grady. (writer)

'Hello, hello,' she breathed into his face. She kissed the air behind his ear, one side then the other. Then back to his mouth. Into his nose. 'Hhhhello, hhhhhello,' she breathed.

'Your breath smells,' said Kevin.

There was a brief moment of nothing.

Then, with a shriek as loud as her mother's when she had told her she wouldn't marry David Gotlieb the trouser manufacturer, Ivy threw up her arms and started to walk backwards. What is more, she was unable to stop either shrieking or stumbling backwards. When she reached the group by the window, it parted like the Red Sea. Ivy continued her clumsy backward march onto the balcony, over the balcony.

Kevin stood very still for quite a long time, staring at the space Ivy had occupied only a minute before. Then he became aware of the sea of faces, jaws moving but with the sound switched off.

Any moment they would move, en masse, talons out, towards him.

He rushed down to the pavement to look for the body of the woman he had killed.

He ran towards the lift, but recoiled in horror to be stuck in it again. No, safer to use the emergency stairs. Fifteen, fourteen, down to the ninth floor. By the seventh floor he became aware of three men coming up. There was something wrong with their faces. No, they were wearing masks, peaked caps with plastic noses. They blocked his way.

'So, matey. Where's the key?'

'What key?'

'What key? The key to the safe.'

'Don't know what you're talking about.'

One produced a gun.

'I don't know what you're talking about,' repeated Kevin, his lips frozen with horror.

The gun was pressed hard into his ribs.

'Take us to it – now.'

'It's, it's in the next building.' Kevin was thinking quickly.

'Take us.'

They went in a tight group down to the busy foyer. The gun pressed painfully into Kevin's ribs every step of the way. The doors parted obligingly, and they were in the street.

'Please God, send help,' Kevin muttered. He did.

The ground floor of the next building belonged to a vet. Drawn into the pavement was an enormous Rolls-Royce. The door was open wide and in it was jammed a plump elderly woman with an elderly dog in a frilly basket.

'I'm stuck, I'm stuck,' she appealed to Kevin. 'Can you help me with Elsie? Please, please, can you?'

Kevin looked enquiringly at the chauffeur.

The chauffeur tipped his peaked cap. 'Sorry, mate.'

'Luis has a bad back,' she implored. 'Do help me.'

'Of course, I'll carry the basket right into the vet for you.' The gunmen let him go.

Safely inside, he peered out through the window.

They were out there. Waiting for him.

Kevin managed to slip out to the back of the premises, passing cages of pet animals in various stages of repair. He found a back door, which led to a yard. Grim and grey, with waste bins and a high wall.

He dragged the bins, clawed at the wall in desperation, and ripped his jacket in several places. The filthy wall covered his suit in black stains. Still he strained and pulled until, to his relief, he reached the top, and toppled over like a rag doll.

Kevin lay stunned for one moment.

Then, slowly, air started to leak into his lungs.

Wiping a lump of mud from his face, he gingerly felt to see if any of his limbs were broken.

No. They seemed all right. The only reason his sleeve was hanging down was because it was torn out of his jacket.

He had fallen onto a well-hidden nest of eggs and they now made an interesting pattern with the greasy black stains down his front.

Breaking and cracking his way through the labyrinth of twigs and leaves, he finally emerged from an elder-berry bush.

To confront Veronica Saunders.

Veronica Saunders. Legs well firmed by years on the playing field. In the gym. In the swimming pool. Veronica was a good all-rounder, and sports mistress at St Mary's Junior School for Girls.

Now she stood like a dragon belching fire, brandishing a hockey stick, her face screwed up like a deflating crimson balloon.

Behind her, clinging in one terrified lump were the members of Class 4B.

Forty seven-year-olds. Eighty wide open eyes. Eighty hands clinging desperately onto the next.

Veronica exploded.

'You little shit. Murderer. Scum of the earth,' she muttered. 'Breaking into schools. Innocent children are the victims. You bastards read about it in the papers and think you can do the same.'

When class 4B heard 'innocent children', that was it. One started to wail and it was quickly taken up by the rest until their cries ripped through the air.

'Thought you could creep in the back way, did you? Come one step nearer and you get this hockey stick in your ear hole.'

The cries of the children rose to even greater heights.

Veronica shouted even louder, 'You've had it, scum,' and blew her whistle. 'Call the police. Call the police,' she shouted to the frightened ones that came running out of the school.

⚜

'What's he done?' asked the sergeant.

'Threatened a school, sarge.'

'Christ. Shove him in.'

Kevin was bounced into his cell in a manner suitable for a child molester.

⚜

The judge spoke for an hour on the perils of present-day society, saying that it was villains like this who caused anguish and sorrow throughout the world. Kevin, fearing he had killed the novelist, stayed quiet. If the judge had his way Kevin would be hung. As it was, all he could give was twelve months.

In all the excitement of being arrested, being kept in a cell and going to prison, Kevin failed to see a daily paper. So how was he to know that for three days one story had dominated the headlines? A very famous novelist, Ivy O'Grady, had catapulted out of a sixteenth-floor window at the Plaza Centre, and lived. She had been caught in the sun canopy of the coffee lounge on the fourth floor, and hundreds of shoppers had gazed skywards at the one fat leg sticking through the green and white striped awning.

It had taken several firemen to lift her to safety, then to a private ward filled with enough flowers for a royal funeral. Her broken ankle was plastered high into the air.

Ben was delighted. It was just the publicity they needed.

'This will sell 'em,' he chuckled and lit another cigar.

❀

'I killed a woman,' Kevin told his cellmate.

'What d'ya get for that?'

'I dunno. Nobody's mentioned it yet.'

His cellmate dug into the bit of wood he was whittling.

Kitty came to see him. She brought her crochet with her. She was making a new chair-back cover for when he came home.

'You won't know the flat,' she told him.

'I killed a woman, Ma,' he whispered.

'And I got you a new bed while I was at it.'

'Did I need one, Ma?'

'I thought so, that old one was no good for your back.

Oh, and while they were at it I said we'll have new carpets as well. Dark red it is, nice colour, hope you like it.'

Next time Kitty came, she brought good wishes from everyone in the tower block. And a fountain pen and pencil set made of gold.

'What's this for, Ma?'

'It's for your birthday.'

'It looks like gold.'

'It is.'

'I usually have a ball point.'

'That'll help you with your writing.'

'Why are you wearing that ring, Ma? You never wore rings, Ma.'

'That's right, son. But Belinda thought they were a good idea. Help my image she said.'

'Who's Belinda?'

'She calls herself a PR, works for this magazine company. She's no bigger than a three-penny bit. Skirt up to her arse. But she's all there. She puts me right.'

'What's happening? Why have you got all this money?'

'It's a long story. I'll tell you next time,' and Kitty rolled up her crochet and got up to leave.

❦

'I did kill a woman you know,' Kevin repeatedly told his cellmate.

'All right, all right, why don't you take up smoking – or playing darts?'

⚜

'They seem to think you'll be out soon,' said Kitty.

'I killed a woman, Ma.'

'I'm sure you did love. But that's why you're likely to be out. Your social lady calls it a common delusion, and all you need is help, and she's gonna give it to you. What you need is a good holiday, and I'm planning one for you.'

'Where's the money coming from, Ma?'

'I don't know, it just floats towards me. You see. It all started when you got yourself arrested. It was in all the papers.'

'I didn't see it.'

'You wasn't allowed to, it was part of the treatment. Anyway, the morning after your arrest, I woke up to find the walkway filled with photographers and paper people and all that.'

'Journalists?'

'Yes. An' they were all asking me questions and scribbling in pads, and flashing their cameras until I was blinded, I hadn't even had me cornflakes. I couldn't think, I didn't really know what you'd done; I didn't know what to do. So, I just shouted out, "What will be will be," and started to shut the door. One young bloke put his foot in the door, he was sweating. He raised his pen, and very politely said, "What is your name, madam?" So I said, "Well, it's, it's . . ." "Madam?" says he. "Yes," I said. "Madam er, er . . ." And do you know, I just couldn't say Brown. It just didn't seem important enough in front of all that mob. So I started to think, Brown. Now what's brown? Sugar, I thought. I could see Barbados, dark sugar.'

'So?'

'So I said "Sugar", and he said, "Thank you, Madam Sugar," and that's what they called me in the papers. There was a great big picture of me with the cat and me nightcap on me head an' it said: *Madam Sugar says, 'What has to be will be.'*

'And then?'

'That's when Belinda took me over. She made me wear Indian-type frocks and big jewellery. I crocheted one of me hats and one firm ordered hundreds of 'em.'

'Did they pay you?'

'Oh yes. Belinda saw to that. I soon had people coming in big cars from foreign countries coming for advice.'

'What did you tell 'em?'

'Oh things like, "A stitch in time saves nine," and that

one that goes, "For the want of a shoe a horse was lost, For the want of a horse the battle was lost," and so on, you know.'

'Everybody knows them Ma. Granny used to say those things all the time.'

'I know, but they don't. They're only kids. It doesn't matter what you say. Just say it slowly, and people will believe you. I've got to go now. I've got to get on with me column.'

'You've got a column?'

'Oh yes, Madam Sugar's column is famous now. Belinda helps me with it a bit, but I always think up a wise saying.'

'Like?'

'Like "All's well that ends well".'

And it did. Kevin emerged from prison in his tatty, torn once pea-green suit. Belinda was there to greet him. She shook his hand warmly. 'It's lovely to meet the son of the great Madam Sugar.'

Kevin was confused. His year in prison had left him uneasy with the social graces, and now he found himself staring speechlessly at this vivacious young woman. Suddenly, words stuttered from his frozen lips.

'How happy I am this day to meet you. Take my hand and let me greet you.'

Belinda stood transfixed.

'What was that?' she whispered.

'This must be my lucky day, the one in which you came my way,' replied Kevin, loosening up a little.

'Oh Kevin, you are just what I want!'

'I am?'

'Yes, yes, Kevin – for our birthday and bereavement card department. We are sadly short of ode writers and sales are flagging. Our sales department needs you, Kevin. Please, will you join us?'

'I have the very thing,' said Kevin, and he took out his golden pen.

Christine

One day, when she was fifty-nine, Doris sat in front of her triple-mirror dressing table and decided she was getting old.

'You're getting on a bit,' she said to her reflection. 'You never saw one like this, did you, Frank? Not with this old wrinkly face.'

She looked down into Frank's face.

Frank, trapped in his silver frame, looked back at her with the same grin he had given her at the Rotary Club ball. Twenty-five years ago.

He was still holding the splendid cigarette box, his prize for excellence in pyrotechnics. Frank had owned a fireworks factory. Not a big one, in fact, quite a small one, in an old stable block across the lawn, down the side path and into the yard.

'Expand, expand, Frank,' his friends would say. 'You're a good businessman. You could go for the major stuff. Coronations. New Years, war endings and whatnot.'

But Frank would just dip his head in that endearing way he had, and smile. 'No! No! It's fine. Enough's enough.'

For at the back of his mind was his big comfortable home, his big comfortable bank balance and his big comfortable income. All was right with the world. Leave it alone.

Doris ran his home in a fashion which suited both of them. A bit disorganized. A bit untidy. So they drifted through life together not caring about anyone else's opinion. The only criticism came from their daughter, Christine. And that was a wordless observation. Christine had a way of tightening her lips. At the same time there was a hardness about her eyes which turned them from a soft blue-grey to darkest charcoal in colour.

They had laughed too loud at a parents' evening when she was in the sixth form. They had dressed in a vulgar manner for a school concert. Well, Doris knew she had offended when she was only trying to do her daughter proud. She had bought the fake leopard-skin coat especially for the occasion, but it went into the jumble-sale bag at the back of the wardrobe along with the rest of the things that had received the thumbs down.

She knew it wasn't Frank. Nothing wrong with Frank. Just a nice quiet dad in a good overcoat.

'Do you think Christine will grow out of it?' she quizzed Frank on the way home.

They had pulled into a lay-by to eat their fish and chips. The passing traffic lit her with flashes of light. Her lips were greasy with the careless way she had of eating.

Frank slapped the oily newspaper into a ball and tossed it into the hedge. 'Course she will, duckie. She's growing up. She's at a sensitive age just now.' He inhaled deeply on a cigarette. The car was filled with the combined perfume of vinegar and smoke.

'I think we're both a bit frightened of her, Frankie.'

'You could be right, gel. You could be right.' And he slid the car out of the lay-by.

❀

'And, d'you know, Frankie, she's just like that today. I'm still frightened of her. In fact, I'm more frightened of her now she's forty and I haven't got you around to back me up. I know you're still there, Frank.'

She kissed his smiling face. 'I miss you, love.'

❀

'I've been for a walk, Frankie. I've been to the old graveyard. It's nice there. It's peaceful. You'd like it.'

Doris, in her usual fashion, slipped off her stockings and hung them on the banister rail. Her jumper draped on one easy chair, her skirt on another. She poured herself a glass of sherry and sprawled on the brocade sofa.

'That woman was there again I told you about. Bit down on her luck she is. Rents a room from the man who makes false teeth on the sly. Works in that shop where I got my padded bra when I had my breast off. Mrs Traviss her name is. Did I tell you, Frankie?'

After a cheese and pickle sandwich washed down by one more sherry, she felt strangely elated. She opened the French doors into the side garden. The rain had stopped and the warm, pungent smell of the earth was perfume. She stepped out into the shadows. She felt the wet grass on her bare feet. On the radio, a tango played.

Hanging her wig on the lawnmower, Doris began to dance. A sensuous movement on the cool, wet grass.

In the morning, Christine rang.

'Ivan can't stay late. He has a big case on Monday. So it could only be tea. Anyway, the children mustn't be late in bed. It's hard getting them up for school. Ophelia has had too many parties lately and is feeling rather tired. I took her to see Dr Long on Tuesday and he says she's fine, but to keep up the iron foods, after all, she is a girl. Make sure Will cleans the sandpit in case they want to play. Shall I bring sandwiches?'

'Oh no, let me do them. I'll make egg ones for the children.'

'Make sure the eggs are organic.'

'I always do, Christine, and . . .'

Doris danced
on the wet grass.

'I've got some smoked salmon left from the bridge party.'

'I thought . . .'

'I'll bring what's left of the cake.'

'Let me get a cake, I'd like to get . . .'

'Bye-bye, Momma. See you Sunday. God bless.'

❦

Doris loved shopping. Having endured the anxiety of entertaining Christine and her family to tea, she felt she deserved a treat. She decided to go to the emporium, maybe buy a vest. The underwear department was in the basement of the vast, crumbling building. The store was built by Adolphus Damp in 1890 for the sale of 'Goods from the British Empire' and now reeked with the odour of dust and decay.

Happily settled on a chair with Mrs Traviss on the opposite side of the counter, Doris played with the underwear. Contentment wrapped around her like a warm blanket. She felt she could chatter without fearing she had said something foolish, and the only chance of being disturbed was if someone passed through to use the staff lavatory.

'Do you get a tea break, Mrs Traviss?'

'Oh yes. There are strict rules about that.'

'What about . . .' Doris' voice sank to a whisper. 'What about going to the toilet?'

'No worry about, that Mrs Stone. I've got Alice here. We share duties.'

'Alice?'

'Yes, she's there on the sewing machine.'

'I don't see her.'

'I expect she's asleep at the moment, she'll be along.'

Awakened by the sound of their voices, Alice moved towards them in a haze of Vicks VapoRub. She instantly took to Mrs Stone. She warmed to the bold colours of her dress and felt she could quite happily lean against that vast figure, for Alice was a tired person.

Alice was in her seventies, but looked older. As small and frail as a bird, her deeply furrowed face was touched with make-up at the high points. Her scrag of hair burned bright with henna.

She looked at Doris with a smile of incredible sweetness and held out her hand. 'It's a rest for me, working here, you see, Mrs Stone. A resting place after all me travels. I've had to knock around a lot. Just to earn me living and send a bit home to Mummy.'

'Where did you knock around, Alice?'

'The camps.'

'Camps?'

'Yes, you know, holiday camps. They were everywhere. I went round 'em all.'

'What did you do, Alice?'

'Tidying ashtrays mostly. It's a full-time job, Mrs Stone. They fill up the minute you empty 'em. It's essential work, Mrs Stone. Essential.'

'I've had such a nice day today,' Doris told Frankie later as she slipped between the sheets. 'Two lovely people at the emporium. I feel I've made a friend.' She stroked the silver frame before she kissed it.

❁

Christine sat with Doris by the river. She had been with her mother for her check-up. Now they were sharing a pot of tea. Each had a lemon tart on a small white plate.

'So, here we are,' said Christine.

'Isn't it nice?'

'Just look. Over there. That's the National Theatre.'

'Fancy that.'

'You could do this yourself. Any day. Have a cup of tea.'

'Yes.'

'I mean it, Momma. Have a day out.'

'Yes.'

A pause.

'So, Momma. Was the doctor pleased with you? Really?'

'Oh yes. No sign, he said. No sign at all.'

'So, you will live for ever?'

'On no, Christine. I won't.'

'Momma, how can you say such a thing, today, when you've had the all-clear?'

'Well, they did take my blood pressure as well, and that's way up. So's my cholesterol. No, they told me I could drop dead any minute.'

'Do take more care of your diet, Momma. What would I do without my mummy? What would the children do without their granny? They adore you. Now, come and see the paintings.'

'Can I have another lemon tart?'

'No.'

Immediately she returned home, Christine rushed up the stairs to her bedroom. Dived to the back of the wardrobe and pulled out a sober, black, two-piece suit, checked it for moths and made sure the black-edged handkerchief was in place.

Satisfied, she pushed it back again behind her bright frocks, to await the funeral.

❦

'We'd been to Clacton for the day.'

Doris wove her way around the gravestones.

'We were watching these men. They weren't half having a smashing time. All jumping up and down in the water. As they came up they all shouted "Fuck oh fuck".

Because they all felt happy I suppose. Frankie started to laugh. It looked so funny. He threw his head back. Then he coughed. He always kept a nice clean hankie in his pocket. When he looked down at it, there was blood. He was dead two months later.

'When I was a youngster, I worked in his fireworks factory, you know. We were having it off in the storeroom. But then I fell for Christine.

'Have you got any children, Mrs Traviss?'

'A son.'

'D'you see him?'

'No.'

'Where does he live?'

'He sent me a card from America a few years ago, but there was no return address.'

❧

Christine sat at the kitchen table with Val. Val was her closest friend. Tall, angular Val worked at a stray animal shelter in Walthamstow. As a sideline she had a mail-order catalogue. This is what the pair of them studied now. Christine always bought a few things from the catalogue. Just to help Val. She wouldn't dream of wearing them, so just shipped them off to the charity shop.

'My mother could do with a dress like that,' said Christine. 'She always looks such a mess. Did I tell you she makes smoked salmon sandwiches with white bread?'

'Yes.'

'Thick soft rubbish white bread.'

'Yes.'

When Val had gone, Christine got out the air freshener and scented the space where Val had been sitting. There was, she believed, a faint smell of cat.

⚙

It was a warm evening. Doris took off her wig and sauntered into the side garden in her petticoat, danced a few steps then turned to look at the house. She had forgotten the door there. It was covered in ivy now.

It was the garden door to the old pantry. Good size rooms. Big windows. It could be a flat. It would be better for Mrs Traviss than that little tiny bedroom with a po under the bed.

Doris sat on the lawnmower for quite a long time, thinking about it.

Then she went to the phone.

⚙

Christine had gathered all the plants on the table and was washing the leaves with milk. Val was studying the mail-order catalogue. The front door clicked.

Christine washes the plants with milk

'Ivan, Ivan,' Christine shrieked down the hall. 'Ivan, come and say hello to Val. Val's here. We're choosing things. Ivan, where are you? What are you doing?'

'I'm in the cloakroom,' Ivan yelled.

'Don't make a smell in there. Val may want to go.'

'I don't,' moaned Val.

'There's a nice spray in there,' confided Christine. 'Lily of the valley. Men are a bit messy anyway.'

Ivan emerged into the kitchen and threw a vague, off-hand greeting into the air. 'Tea?' he said.

'Make some,' said Christine.

Ivan popped tea bags into mugs, but before he got to the hot water, the phone rang. Ivan answered it and talked lawyer-speak for a few minutes, then dropped the gadget back in the slot.

'Who was that?'

'It was your mother.'

'My mother?'

'Yes.'

'Why didn't you hand it to me?'

'She didn't ask to speak to you.'

'Surely she was ringing me?'

'No. She wanted to speak to me.'

'What for?'

'To ask my advice.'

'About what?'

'Property.'

'Property?'

'Yes. You know, alterations, conversions, permissions to be granted.'

'Granted for what?'

'For turning rooms into a flat.'

'A flat in her house? A flat in her house?' Christine stood upright, her head dropped back as if to be crucified. 'You know what this means?' she cried. 'You know what this means? A flat for that woman. That woman from that shop will go and live there. Then the old bat will die. And I will inherit the house. Not with vacant possession, but with a woman . . . a person living . . . living . . .'

Great gasps of air interrupted her flow of words which were sucked back into her throat. She staggered backwards, clenched fists beating the air. Then, like a spring, she bounced forward to the table and viciously started sweeping the pots onto the floor.

Earth scattered over the immaculate whiteness of everything. An orchid in flower cracked as it hit the dishwasher.

Ivan and Val moved in like automatons. Silently and efficiently, a paper bag was placed over Christine's head. They led her, moaning, off to her room with a good supply of frozen peas.

Ophelia and Adam sniggered through the door crack as she passed them on the landing.

The sound of the bathroom woke her. The peas on her head were melted and warm, the pillow was damp.

'Is that you, Ivan?'

'Who else? Go back to sleep. It's late.'

'How late?'

'Gone midnight.'

'Where have you been?'

'Well, I had to give Val a lift home, didn't I?'

'I suppose so, I suppose so . . . Ivan . . .?'

'Shut up. I'm knackered.'

⚘

Christine rang.

'Mummy dear, you know you will have a birthday soon?'

'Yes.'

'And you know you're going to be sixty? Well, it's a big one, and we want to celebrate it in style. Take you to the Ritz for dinner.'

Doris was thrilled. She hadn't been to the Ritz since Frankie had died.

Outfits were flung all over the place as unsuitable. Finally she chose a plain dark chiffon with a string of good pearls. She felt a glow when she saw approval on Christine's face after her swift inspection.

She enjoyed her dinner but wished she had not drunk

LIZ SMITH

quite as much. She couldn't quite remember what she had eaten, Ivan had filled her glass so often.

She relaxed on the elegant sofa with her coffee.

'Aren't the carpets pretty?'

'They're all right,' answered Christine. 'A bit old-fashioned now.'

Doris felt crushed, she decided to enjoy the prettiness of the place in silence. If only she could see it. It was floating a bit. Surely that was a lot of brandy to have with her coffee, yet here was Christine pushing her to have more. More of everything. The chandeliers melted together and became one. Christine spoke through the mist.

'So, did you see Dr Long this week, Momma?'

'Oh yes. Still go regularly.'

'Everything OK?'

'As usual, you know. Blood pressure up. Cholesterol up. It's the same every time. I'm used to it now. I could drop dead any minute.'

'Now don't say that, Mummy. Even in fun. But . . .'

'But what?'

'You're going to be with us a few years yet, please God. But . . . but, if . . . if anything should happen, it won't of course, but do you realize how much tax would be taken?'

Doris really felt in need of sleep. She didn't want to think about taxes.

'Mummy, Mummy. Have you ever thought of turning the house over to me?'

'Turn the place over to you?'

'Only in my name, it would take a burden off your shoulders.'

'Would it?' Doris wished she didn't feel so fuddled. But felt she would agree to anything, just to be able to walk towards the door without falling over.

That night Doris held the silver frame closely to her for a very long time before she fell asleep.

'Frankie, oh Frankie, if only you were here to advise me. She says I won't know any different. Ivan can fix it up so it will all be fine for me, but the house will already be hers when I die. Look after me, darling boy.'

During the days that followed, Doris wandered around the house, touching the walls, stroking the marble fireplaces. Turning the taps on and off in the kitchen. It all felt the same. Just the same. Christine said it would.

She sat in the side garden and thought and thought about it, looking at the door to the old pantry which could never now be a separate flat.

She would smarten the place up a bit for Christine. Yes, that's what she would do now. She wouldn't half be pleased to inherit a house all put to rights. She liked things put to rights, did Christine.

❀

It had been raining all day. A relentless grey sheet of solid rain. Dark from the very beginning. Early February. Bitterly cold.

Christine awoke to find herself alone in the house. Ivan, having a court appointment in deepest Kent, had left at some ungodly hour. She remembered that. Ophelia was using her gap year to study housing and crime in the East End, and usually took Adam to school on her way.

She called their names but they had gone. Why the silence?

Mrs Carter usually woke her when she hoovered the landing.

The rain spat against the windows. Mrs Carter rang to say she had a bad back. She would have to get her own breakfast now.

'Damn! Damn! Damn!' shouted Christine to the dark and silent hallway. She had depended on her coming today. Typical of her to let her down. 'Stupid. Stupid bitch,' she groaned. 'She knew it was my turn to do the bridge lunch.'

But that was not to be.

One by one they rang. Diana couldn't come. She was terrified of storms and would spend the rest of the day under the bedclothes, clutching her dog.

Damn. Damn. Damn.

Celia rang and said her car was out of order.

Doreen came. She would, of course. Through hell and high water, Doreen would come. She had nothing to say, but said it at great length. On the sofa, opposite, Christine felt her face grow numb. She was sure she slept but as she woke, Doreen's lips were still moving. She leaped to the door when Doreen said it was time to go.

Back in the hallway she kicked the bronze flowerpot, hurting her toe. Christine gave a howl of despair. 'What a day,' she said to the big fat satin cushion on the sofa. 'What a bloody awful day. It couldn't get worse.'

But it did.

She pushed her head against the cushion and tweaked her hair until she fell into an uneasy sleep. When she awoke, it was quite dark. The telephone was ringing. At first she could not be sure of the message. It was a voice with a foreign accent. Not easy to understand. She asked the caller to repeat. And again.

It was from a hospital, far away, in south London, over the river, near Peckham. It was as if the call came from outer space. It was to say that Ivan had been involved in an accident with his car. Nothing serious. He had hurt his leg, not badly, but they would keep him in for observation for a couple of days. Visiting hours were until 8 p.m.

They gave her the address. She found it on the *A to Z*. It seemed easier to go to the moon.

The rain pounded on the roof of her car like the beat of African drums. Christine edged the car carefully down the Finchley Road. She could see the blurred outline of the traffic through the streaming windows.

'Come on. Get out of my way! I've got to get to some god-forsaken place in south London.'

Why did he have to have the accident there? It should have been round here, then I could easily get to the Royal Free, she thought. Push forward a little, good. Then, not good. An accident in St John's Wood had created a diversion. The bright yellow mac of a policeman approached her window. He signalled she had to go. She made the detour along with a parade of helpless cars.

Look at the time. How could it be that time? Such a long way to go. But she had to wait her turn in the slow procession. Edge around, get into Baker Street, crawl into Park Lane. Slowly over the river to a land that felt so alien it could have been Mars. Resentfully she made her way through the unfamiliar streets. Stupid idiot. Fancy having an accident in a place like this. Typical of him.

Coping as best she could with one-way streets and every traffic light flashing red, she crawled into the area of the hospital. Not far now. Somewhere round here. It was already half past seven. There would be very little time left to see Ivan. Enough perhaps to give him his clean pyjamas and ask when he would be home.

It was a quarter to eight when she passed through the doors of the rather shabby hospital. A quick enquiry at the desk and she was running towards the ward. It was a big ward. Where was Ivan? Not easy to see, people were leaving, getting in her way. Clumsy morons. Quickly she looked from right to left. No familiar face. Was that a big cage over Ivan's hurt leg? She went towards it. She looked over the cage and saw Ivan's head on the pillow beyond. But, more amazingly, resting on Ivan's chest was another head. It was Val's head. It was Val lying across her beloved in perfect harmony which was reflected in their faces.

For one moment, Christine was paralysed. But only for a moment. Then, with a strangled scream she threw the clean pyjamas into Ivan's face.

The two of them stared speechless and listened to the tirade. She ebbed down to a hoarse whisper. A nurse asked her to leave.

'So,' she croaked. 'All those journeys to Walthamstow, all those lifts home you were reluctant to take. That's why you took so long?'

They agreed. It had been going on a long time.

'How could you? You creep. Carrying on in that little house with your old granny there.'

'My old granny is stone-deaf and sleeps heavily,' said Val, in a rather matter-of-fact way.

❀

The divorce was very straightforward. Ivan saw to everything. A few minutes in the law courts in the Strand and their long-ago promises to each other were all melted away.

Christine changed her will in favour of her children and Ivan bought her a very nice flat far north of Golders Green. She would have no financial worries.

'Guilt,' said Christine, slamming the door of her new BMW.

Doris, standing on the step to say farewell, felt tired and funny after a long and wearisome dialogue on the wrongs and deceit of the guilty pair. She longed to get back to planning how to get rid of her present sofa and acquire the new one she had seen yesterday in Harrods. Before Christine's car was out of sight, Doris was back, happily worrying with a fresh cup of tea.

Although Christine was satisfied with her new home, it brought her little joy. She found herself sitting for hours in the large comfortable lounge looking at the busy road beyond the far-off hedge. A strip of grass ran between the building and the road, cut down within an inch of its life. If a daisy dared to show it was beheaded immediately.

Christine sprays the chair where Val has been

What I need now, she thought, is a different life. What I need now is glamour. It would be better when her engagements started again. It was time for the reminder slips: her committees, bridge parties, charity lunches. But the invitations did not come. She was a single woman. A danger.

She must make a new life. Of course, she needed a man. She needed a man for all kinds of reasons. For sex. For companionship. To go on holiday with. Not to have to walk into a restaurant alone. To have a different opinion on everything. She wondered what he would be like. Unlike the men she had known, he would wear a leather jacket and denim trousers and would drive a Porsche. The thought of him gave her a frisson of excitement, and she poured herself another glass of whisky.

She rarely saw the children now. Ophelia preferred to share a flat with friends. Adam crept in with her. He enjoyed the sardine-packed, noisy place. They each had a room in her new flat, but seemed to regard it as a place to store things. They would only appear if they needed a book or a piece of clothing. Then, having picked up the required article, they would slide out of the door. Anxious to leave.

Because of the difficulties of parking, Christine wondered what it was like to travel on a bus. That was how she discovered the market in Camden.

Why, she thought, had she never discovered this place before? She had lived all these years in Hampstead, just up the hill, she had known all about it, knew it was there, but had never visited. How lacking in colour, how narrow was her old life. How she would expand it now. There was so much to discover. The whole world was waiting for her to find it.

Her neighbours were so quiet they hardly seemed to be living there. No, she had to seek beyond the anonymity of the roads streaming with the incessant movement of unknown people going to unknown places. She wanted to be part of a more exciting life where contact with like-minded people was instant, where people lay around on sofas smoking funny-smelling cigarettes, talking art and philosophy then going for long walks together, or just having meals which went on for ever and where the table got very untidy. Of course, there would be lots and lots of sex.

Christine burned at the thought of it, and had another glass of whisky.

She was drawn endlessly to the fantasy shops. Most of all she wanted the exotic garments made of black rubber; they seemed to express all she wanted from her new life, because they would take her to strange places. But where would those places be? She had to find out. There was no one to stop her. No one to give astonished looks at her extraordinary choice of outfit: black rubber, a basque and long suspenders. For her throat, a bold necklace of black jet holding a large bat of crimson glittering glass. For her disguise, a mask of red leather with a central eye and a single feather. On her wrist, a chunky bracelet composed entirely of safety pins.

She viewed herself in the hard and pitiless light of the bathroom. 'I am someone else,' she said aloud. 'Someone I want to be.'

Her heart beat with excitement at the sight of the strange, exotic creature she saw in the mirror. She felt transported. Elated. This fascinating, unfamiliar figure she saw before her was her very own self. A stranger. Yet not a stranger. It had been there all the time. This new person belonged only to her. Now she had to find out what to do with her.

She was surprised at the respectability of the magazine wherein she found the name of the nightclub that obviously offered the experience she was seeking.

❦

It was with a beating heart that she got out of the taxi.

She was taken aback to see it was under some railway arches. The night was dark and she felt there must have been a mistake, but the driver pointed to a flashing blue arrow down an alleyway.

A surly doorman asked her for five pounds and a look in her handbag, then pointed her down some stone steps into an area of near-darkness.

Christine found the ladies' lavatory. Once inside the door she was blinded by the colour scheme. Walls cobalt blue, ceiling crimson, doors of crude and crumbling turquoise. Blinking, she became aware of other occupants, two women, locked in a hot embrace.

"Scuse me,' she whispered, and completed her outfit in front of the mottled mirror.

It was with a hopeful heart that she entered the dimly lit bar, thick with strange-smelling smoke, pierced with shafts of coloured light and extremely warm. Which was just as well, as very little clothing was worn. Christine felt overdressed.

In the black-painted interior, a row of near-naked men sat chatting casually at a long bar, sometimes slipping off their stools and drifting off, two by two. It was difficult to tell their age. A pierced nipple and baseball cap can do a lot to disguise it. Some with better bodies wore a jewelled codpiece.

She bought a whisky at a price she felt would have bought a car, and watched the sensuous movements of the dancers on the tiny floor.

A hand came out of the darkness and caressed her breast. She turned, expecting to see a man, but instead found a woman, smiling very close to her face.

'Take your mask off. I'd like to see your face.'

'Er no. Not yet.'

LIZ SMITH

'Aw, come on.' The woman leaned in, pressing her mouth into Christine's face, her breath giving off a stench of rotten teeth and cheap wine.

Christine moved off with revulsion, edging her way to the dance floor. The heat there was visible. She could feel a trickle of sweat stinging behind the mask. She had to remove it. She wiped her face with her arm. As she lifted her head she looked into the faces of a couple dancing slowly by.

'That's better,' said the little fat man, his arms wrapped around his partner.

His companion seemed to be clothed entirely in tattoos. He was taller and much younger, with well-defined muscles.

'You've got a nice face. Show it. My name's Tony by the way, this is my friend Vincent.'

Christine smiled with relief at their goodwill. Suddenly she felt as gauche and awkward as a schoolgirl.

'Now, why haven't we seen you here before, dear?'

'Oh, well, I'm just sort of finding my way around, that's why.'

'Oh! Delayed along the way, were we? Life can be a bit hard on a girl, can't it, ducky?'

Christine felt her defences slipping. She found the little fat man with the sweaty skin and smeared make-up quite repulsive.

'Your glass is empty.' Tony took a swift sniff. 'Whisky, you like whisky. Very upmarket, dear. Vince, go and get her another one, bring one for me.'

With his friend departed, Tony turned to her. 'I think you're lovely, dear. I have a feeling we could be mates. You've got a lonely look. I'm good like that, you know. I'm understanding. A bit psychic you might say. My old mum always says "He's a fairy". You'd like my old mum. You'll like me when you get to know me, duckie.'

Tony picked up her hand and batted it with his own sweaty paw. His meanness and the mixture of sweat and perfume filled her with a sudden panic. She leaped to her feet in order to go. But he was in front of her, his arms around her and his fat belly pressed into her.

'Don't go yet. We hardly know each other.'

'I must get some air.'

She was stopped in her tracks by his sudden onslaught. One arm tightened around her, the other hand desperately searched her crotch, his mouth moved over hers and his sinewy tongue shot down her throat like a snake. The more she pushed away from him, the tighter he pulled. She fought with all her might but only slid over the greasy sweat on his belly. It seemed she could never break free.

Vince returned with the whisky. 'Drinks,' he said laconically, as if he were witnessing nothing.

Tony turned to look at him and Christine fled.

Out into the night Christine ran, wrapped in her overcoat, throwing off her trimmings as she fled. She found the road beyond. There was a drizzle of rain which only emphasized the unreality of it all. She lifted her head into the wet mist and was grateful for it. The road ahead was long. Alien and strange to her. The shops were ugly and unfamiliar. A wet dog ran along the pavement. An all-night bus passed, a few grey faces pressed against the window, as in a dream. Where was it going? Nowhere she knew. Perhaps to some under-world. Hellfire and brimstone. Oh, the strangeness of it all. No taxis. No one in sight. A solitary man approached, wet, on a bike.

'Where am I?'

He looked at her as if she were mad. Then the road was empty again.

Her tears began to mingle with the rain. She limped along in dancing shoes, then at the high point of her despair, she saw a light. A shop was still open. It was a small bar. A glass of water would do, just to rinse the filthy taste out of her mouth.

A heavily pregnant girl, about fourteen years old, was playing a game. An old man was asleep in a chair. A Chinese woman put her head around an inner door. She was cleaning her teeth.

'Can I have a coffee? Please.'

The coffee appeared.

'Want something in it?' The woman pushed her tooth-brush down into her jumper.

'Isn't it after time?'

'Nobody comes round here. Nobody.'

'I'd be grateful for a brandy.'

'You look done in, rest yourself.'

'When do you close?'

'We don't much. There'll be more in later.'

When Christine opened her eyes, there were more people. And he was there. He was standing by the counter. He was jovial, confident. He was in charge. He wore a leather jacket and denim trousers and his name was Trevor. She could hear that. His companions, eager to speak to him, addressed him constantly.

He was the man of her dreams. He looked exactly as she had imagined and she knew instinctively that he drove a Porsche.

He must turn towards her.

He did.

❦

Christine sat on her sofa and could hardly believe her good luck. Now she was content just to be there waiting to be called, for this was her new life. The life she had dreamed of. So strange the way it had come about. So unexpected. If I'd not had that peculiar desire to dress in all that weird gear I would never have been down there, she mused. So what put that into my head? I must have an angel watching over me.

It all led to this. To her new life with Trevor. Well, not exactly with him, not all the time. He still lived in his Spitalfields flat. She still lived in hers. It was the same flat, but it had taken on a new aura. The stream of traffic outside the window had taken on a new meaning; it was going somewhere. The miserable strip of grass had an occasional dandelion. She pulled one and put it in an egg cup. It reminded her that Trevor never had any flowers. That was one of his funny quirks. She had taken him some, to surprise him. There was no vase, so she had put them in a jug. She expected a smile of surprise, but he had exploded in anger, swept them onto the floor where the jug shattered.

'Leave the bloody flowers where they belong, in the garden.'

No explanation. Nothing. He was like that with a lot of things. He would sometimes brush her aside when she tried to embrace him. Yet, at odd times in the day, he would ring her to come round at once, tear her clothes off her as she came through the door, then pin her down anywhere. On the kitchen table, the floor, the bed.

She was not quite sure whether she would have liked a more regular relationship or enjoyed the erratic style of this one. There was the attraction of it being different. It wasn't a bit like living with Ivan. That's what they're like, she thought, in his kind of life. Not that she quite understood exactly what his kind of life was.

Trevor was at home a great deal. He had some rather odd-looking friends who always seemed to hang around. He kept a little boat down on the Essex marshes. He was a good sailor and seemed to take regular trips to France. He owned the little bar where she had found him, and seemed to have several more. But Trevor was ambitious. He was working hard towards opening a bigger bar. He talked endlessly of his plans.

'It reminds me of the old movies,' said Christine. 'All glitter and girls in wonderful costumes doing a Busby Berkeley number.'

'That's exactly the idea, that's what I want it to be, but with pole dancers. Right up to date. With class. Real class. A five star chef. The best wines. People will be proud to say they've been there.'

In his excitement he rolled her over on the bed, but fell asleep before he could undo her bra.

So their erratic relationship continued. Her old life seemed far away. Two years, yet it seemed an age.

Trevor's plans materialized. In the shape of an old warehouse, not far from the river.

'It's the place to be. All the toffs work round there. Big bonuses. Spend money like water. Like a bit of glamour after work. I just need a bit of back-up.'

He got it in the bloated form of Baron Greenwell.

The baron had clawed his way from the potato fields of Lincolnshire to a seat in the Lords. And he didn't mind who knew it. Not a bit. 'I've worked hard. I've got my reward. Now I deserve a bit of fun.'

Trevor promised him a lot of fun.

It all went swimmingly, permission was easily granted for everything. Trevor sought her advice. 'You're class, Christine. You're class, you are. I wouldn't have thought about choosing that. Come here. Let's have you.'

'Not here, Trevor.'

But she was pressed against the peeling warehouse wall.

She didn't feel too well when she woke on the morning of the opening night. Better have a quiet day. She didn't want one of those horrible hot flushes. Lie down, have a little drink. Was she drinking too much these days? Today was special, it would help her to see it through. Whisky. Whisky. Have a little sleep.

The telephone woke her. Trevor had to see her.

'Oh no, Trevor. I don't feel like it, I'm not too well.'

'I need it now.'

'No, Trevor. I need to rest.'

'You come now or I'll chuck myself out of the window.'

He was seething with excitement when she arrived, his evening shirt hung on a chair. He laughed a bit. He cried a bit. He opened champagne.

'Oh no,' she cried. 'I've had whisky.'

'Get it down. You want to wish me luck, don't you?'

She drank the champagne.

Later, she sat with the baron on her left. On her right was a man who only showed her his bald head as he turned to his right. The baron kept his head turned towards Trevor whilst his hand holding his stinking cigar waved across her.

Surely, thought Christine, he must put it down when he eats, but to her disgust, he smoked and ate in unison.

The first course arrived. The salmon mousse was as planned but was covered with a strange and pungent sauce, then trimmed with angelica. She groaned. The young chef had read too many articles and was determined to outdo them all.

With each mouthful of food she took in smoke from the cigar.

With the slice of venison, the near-naked waiter offered her limp asparagus and burned roast potatoes from a silver dish, and as he did so she caught a whiff of his sweat and wished he were wearing an apron.

She miserably accepted more wine, automatically drinking it in the absence of a companion to chat with. One sensation after another overwhelmed her. She felt befuddled out of her mind. Her instinct told her to go to the cloakroom immediately, but another part of her brain told her that her legs didn't work. In the haze of the noise, the kaleidoscopic movement of people and smoke, she was aware she had to press down hard on her feet in order to stand upright then make her way to a door she vaguely knew to be there somewhere. With enormous effort and concentration she pressed her feet to the floor and rose. Backwards and forwards she swayed to gain her balance. Backwards and forwards. Now she had to make for the door. Back she drifted again. Then forward. Heavily this time, so that her head seemed to be projected way in front of her body.

At that precise moment, the contents of her stomach rose like a flood and she vomited the whole lot like a fountain on to the table. With head hanging low, she only knew that she felt a whole lot better for being delivered of that burden. She hardly noticed the two heavies arrive on either side of her. She was not aware of them propelling her through the kitchen, and was only vaguely conscious of being thrown out of the back door on to the pile of overflowing rubbish bags. She landed on top of a rat who was happily eating at the time then scurried away, resentful at being disturbed.

It was raining heavily and she opened her lips to it, turning her head to take in her surroundings. She was in the alleyway at the back of the premises, lying in the rain on a heap of garbage, in an evening dress which was getting soaking wet. She couldn't move because she was too drunk. She knew that she could only wait. She felt helpless.

At that moment the door suddenly opened and one of the heavies threw her handbag at her then slammed the door again. That was good; her mobile was in there. Now she could ring Ophelia, to get her out of this mess.

She lay on the greasy bags to wait for her daughter. Out of the darkness came something she took to be a large rat. It did not scurry away but walked over her body with hard feet, smelling the vomit spilled on her dress.

Christine lifted her head and looked into the face of a large cat. An enormous tomcat with ragged ears, a stray whose mangy fur was plastered to his gaunt body in the rain. His face looked inquisitively into hers. In the dim light she could see that, in spite of his parlous state, his eyes were large and glowed like amber.

'Pretty cat,' she murmured. She, who never had a kind word to say of a cat, or any animal for that matter.

She tried to remember who liked cats. Then it came back to her. She'd once had a friend who was good to cats. She was called Val. She used to come to her house in Hampstead. She cared for stray animals. She was a kind person.

With this gentle thought in her mind and the memory of Val, Christine lifted her hand to stroke the starving animal. At that movement of her arm, the cat, with one swift motion, opened wide its mouth and sunk its razor-like teeth into the ball of her thumb.

The pain was hot and fierce. She feebly shook her hand but couldn't dislodge the vice-like grip. Desperately, she summoned energy to use both hands and prise open the fearsome jaws. At first her efforts were of no avail, but gradually the agony added to her strength and the cat gave way.

Ophelia saw her mother to bed and promised to call later in the week. But Christine woke her the following night begging her to come to her because she felt so ill, and there were angry red veins running up her arm, from the injured thumb to the armpit.

Ophelia got her mother to hospital where they did all the good in their power. But within a few hours, Christine was dead.

❀

Doris was sitting, still wearing her dressing gown and drinking tea, contemplating her latest sofa, when the phone rang.

It was Ophelia.

Doris felt a surge of surprise and pleasure. Her granddaughter did not bother to keep in touch very often.

'Hello dear. How nice to hear you. How are you?'

'I'm all right.'

'Are you still at school?'

'University.'

'That's what I meant.'

'It's not about that.'

'Are you wanting something, dear? Money running out?'

'No. Thank you. No. It's about my mother.'

'Christine? Did Christine tell you to ring me?'

'No. She can't.'

'She can't? What d'you mean, she can't?'

'She's had an accident.'

'An accident? What sort of accident?'

'It was a stray cat. She stroked it.'

'A cat? Christine doesn't like cats.'

'She stroked it. It bit her.'

'Oh dear me. Tell her to see a doctor.'

'She did.'

'What did he do about it?'

'He did all he could.'

'So what happened then?'

There was a long pause. Ophelia's voice seemed to come from the end of a long tunnel. 'She died.'

For the time that followed, Doris lived in her separated self. Just moving around in a sense of unreality which took the edge off everything.

Some days, she dressed. Most days, not completely. She roamed, bare-footed, around the place. Sat in the side garden in her petticoat. She managed to get down to the supermarket for a few groceries, and to buy a silver frame for Christine, identical to the one in which Frankie lurked. They sat in their borders, side by side with a little silver vase between them, ever filled with fresh flowers.

Yet she never cried. She had not shed tears since Christine's death; just this strange numbness that removed her from reality. It was a kindly state. It cushioned her against the agony that might have descended. It could have continued indefinitely, but it ended one Sunday afternoon.

Nearly four weeks had passed since the funeral. Doris picked up the newspapers from the hallway.

How heavy they are these days, she whispered to herself.

She made some toast and marmalade, took it, along with a mug of tea, to the sofa. A guilty thought was creeping into her mind. Of late, she had been trying to get the house ready for Christine to inherit: some modern furniture, stripped flooring instead of carpets, plain walls. Doris had found it very uncomfortable but felt Christine would be happier to walk into it. Maybe now she could buy some of her old stuff back. Her big brocade sofa. Carpets again instead of that hard wood. Perhaps, oh yes, a little bit of flowered wallpaper.

But even to continue with that train of thought seemed treason to Christine, and she buried her head in the newspaper. Eventually, realizing she hadn't taken in a single word of what she had read, she allowed the paper to slip, and closed her eyes.

The telephone rang. It was Ophelia.

Once again the instant surge of different emotions at the sound of her granddaughter's voice. Joy that she should ring her. Curiosity about the reason why. It had to be to talk about Christine. They had never really spoken about the way she had died. Doris badly wanted to discuss every detail: Where exactly had the cat come from? Why did it come to Christine? What made Christine stroke the cat? Doris knew it was by the back door of a restaurant, but what was Christine doing there? Doris wanted all the details. She had to rouse herself, get down to the supermarket, buy some Kipling cakes before Ophelia arrived.

Boosted by a sense of mission, she decided to wear her blonde wig. She had lost weight over the past weeks and felt good in her dress.

Maybe she could make some egg sandwiches too. Ophelia had liked them as a child. She had to make sure the eggs were organic, because Christine would have approved. What did Ophelia drink? Perhaps she didn't like tea. Would she like a tinned drink? Would she drink it out of the can as they did on television? Doris desperately wanted to please her granddaughter. She worried so much, that by the time the doorbell rang, her wig was awry and her dress had spills all down the front.

Doris held out her arms, but was coolly swept aside by Ophelia, closely followed by Adam. Surprised, she made a detour to the kitchen to pick up another cup. When she returned, brother and sister were sitting side by side, upright and rigid on the sofa.

Doris poured the tea and they accepted it. She eagerly and clumsily offered the food on the tray, breathlessly listing the choice of whatever they could see before them.

No. They were not eating. A cup of tea was all they required. They hoped she was well.

'Yes. As well as could be expected.'

'Good.'

Was everything all right at school for both of them?

'University.'

'That's what I meant.'

A long pause.

'It seems ages since the funeral.'

A long pause.

'I have mother's ashes in a very nice casket,' said Ophelia, as she sipped her tea.

The conversation was not going the way Doris had hoped. She asked where the ashes might be placed.

'Well,' said Ophelia. 'Here, in the garden.'

'Here?'

'Yes.'

'In this garden?'

'Yes.'

'Oh dear. That makes me feel a bit queer.'

'Why should it?'

'Well, I don't know really, it just makes me feel funny that all that is left of my Christine is under a rose bush by the potting shed.'

Ophelia put her cup down and took a deep breath. 'But you won't be here,' she said.

Doris spilled more tea down her front. Looked up. Perplexed. 'What d'you mean, I won't be here?'

'Just that. You'll be gone.'

'What d'you mean, I'll be gone? Where'll I be gone to?'

'That's not for me to say. The choice is yours. I only know you won't be here.'

'Why won't I be here?'

'I will be here.' Ophelia inclined her head towards her brother. 'We will be here.'

Doris gazed as a rabbit transfixed in headlights.

There was a long deadly silence.

'We have come to accept our inheritance.'

'Inheritance?'

'Don't you remember?' Olivia just refrained from adding, 'you stupid old bitch'. 'Don't you remember when you made everything over to my mother in order to evade tax? Don't you remember that my mother divorced my father, and cut him out of her will, making a new will in favour of her two children?'

'Her two children to inherit?'

'Yes.'

'You?'

'Yes.'

'This was hers wasn't it?'

'Your choice.'

'They talked me into it.'

'The choice was yours, nobody made you.'

'They made it . . . they made it.' Doris began to stumble. Words dropped haphazardly out of her mouth. Finally she managed to say, 'They made it seem the right thing to do, they made it seem I would be foolish not to.'

'It *would* have been foolish not to.'

'It doesn't seem that way. Just look what it's done now.'

'That's because of the turn of events. Who would have thought my mother would die?'

'Why should that make a difference?'

'What d'you mean?'

'Well, even with the house in her name, it was to carry on just as before. She promised me it wouldn't alter anything.'

'Yes, *she* did. When it was hers. She could say whatsoever she liked. But it isn't in her name. She is no longer with us.'

A pause.

'Now it is in *our* name. My and Adam's names. She left everything to us. It has come at an opportune moment. Just when we require it to complete our education.' Ophelia spoke slowly and deliberately, leaving a full stop between each sentence. Waiting a moment for each word to sink in.

Adam sat. Head bent. Nose nearly touching his teacup.

Doris looked around the room as if she expected the walls to embrace her.

'The rent? The rent from the factory?'

'It goes without saying. It's all part of it. We need that for our expenses.' She rose slowly to her feet, putting her empty cup on the tray. 'I think that's all, Grandma. I think you have got the message. I think we should leave now.'

Adam leaped to his feet and scurried to the door.

Ophelia stood still then turned towards her grand-mother. 'Three months,' she said. 'I give you three months.'

A big sob came from Doris' throat. 'Are you completely heartless?'

Ophelia turned again. 'Didn't I come to tell you face to face? I realized it would be too much of a shock to hear it over the phone.' She took a step, then turned again. 'Or in a letter.'

Doris sat on the floor in the debris of her tea party. She tore her wig off, throwing it far into the corner of the room, and her tears flowed. All the tears that had never been, poured and poured from her swollen eyes. All night long she cried. When morning came she was sleepless and exhausted, she could scarcely see across the room with her puffy eyes. But she had returned to herself, the doppelganger had gone. She was in charge of herself. She had a new task to grapple with.

She made some strong tea and rang Mr Day, her lawyer.

❦

'D'you know what he said?'

Mrs Traviss and Alice leaned sympathetically over the

counter. Doris wiped her face with the piled up underwear.

'He said, "Look as much as you like, Mrs Stone. You
just can't afford a retirement flat."'

'And have you looked, Mrs Stone?'

'Well I have, a bit, but it's not easy, there's too many.'

'Too many?'

'They sent me tons and tons of retirement flats.
Thousands of 'em. I didn't know which way to turn.'

'"You can't afford any of 'em," he said. "You'll be left
with about seventy thousand when all is settled. Then
there's the maintenance, not to mention the council tax."'

'And that's always going up,' moaned Alice.

'"You'll have to find an alternative solution to the
problem, Mrs Stone. It is a most unfortunate thing at
your age. Your granddaughter will never relent?"'

'"Hard as nails. Cool as ice," I said. "I'll just keep looking," I said.'

The ladies thought long and hard about her problem.

As soon as she was through the door, Doris picked up
Frankie in his frame, kissed his face slowly and lov-
ingly. 'Put it my way, dearest one. Just put it my way.
What to do. Where to go. Or make your granddaughter
change her mind and act like a human being towards
me.'

But Frankie just smiled, as usual.

❀

Doris was back at the underwear counter, untidying the vests, when little Alice came breathlessly down the stairs into the basement. 'I've been to the lunch club and done my duties,' she announced. 'I've done my clearing, and do you know, when I was tidying round I was swearing at 'em leaving all their bits and pieces. They're an untidy lot. When I found this.' She triumphantly held up a creased newspaper.

'What's that?'

'It's *Loot*, there's everything in here. So I thought, let's have a look. I thought, let's have a look because there might be an idea in here. Why else was it left for me? Have a look, Mrs Stone, dear. Have a look. I've drawn pencil around it. Have a look.'

Doris took the newspaper and looked at the column outlined. She stared at it for a while then lifted her head in disbelief. 'It's caravans,' she said. 'I can't live in a caravan.'

'No, Mrs S. They are not caravans. They are mobile homes.'

'No matter what you call them, they're caravans, Alice. I can't live in a caravan.'

'They are bigger than that, Mrs Stone, dear, and they have bedrooms and a proper bathroom plugged in.'

'They're in the middle of nowhere, lines of them, with a shower room made of tin.'

'Not now, Mrs S. Not now!'

'Made of tin, and painted green.'

'Now why did I think it was fate who left that paper here for me to find?'

'Fate? Not some forgetful old man?'

'No, now listen. One of them mobile homes is in a very nice spot. A very pleasant spot. I've passed it many a time when I went to see my cousin Adolf in Chingford. And I implore you, Mrs Stone, dear, to go and have a look. If it's the only one you do see, have a look at that one.'

To her amazement Doris decided to agree.

It was a balmy morning when Mr Clark called for her in his ancient taxi. Doris kept him waiting.

'Sorry Mr Clark, I just can't hurry today. I don't want to go really.'

'Why *are* you going, missus?'

'It's little Alice. She'd just pester me if I didn't go. It's easier just to do it. Then I can say I've been.'

'Yes.'

Very soon their route took them through avenues of chestnut trees. They left the mean streets behind. From a long, long high road, Mr Clark, as suddenly as his taxi allowed, took a left turn into a narrow lane, stopping by a hole in the hedge.

Wordlessly, Doris looked at him. Wordlessly he nodded.

She got out of the taxi and went slowly towards the gap in the hedge. There she stood, drinking in the scene. A patch of grassy land, surrounded by a tall, wild hedge and trees, enclosing a collection of mobile homes. Seven of them, spread around the perimeter, seven trim and shining little homes, bright with paint and flowers. Each one was set behind its own front garden. Each one had a picket fence, each garden bursting with plants as if trying to rival the one next door.

Doris was transfixed by the scene. She felt she had wandered into another world. The warmth of the sun touched her face, she could hear the bees buzzing about their work, there was a buddleia bush busy with butter-flies, garden gnomes smiled and winked at her, a dog padded up to her, wagging his tail.

She tried to walk forward but her legs couldn't move. No need, a smiling woman came from one of the vans to greet her. 'Hello,' she said. 'Hello.' She held out both her hands. Taking Doris' arm she propelled her towards the little home. 'I'm Mrs Williamson,' she announced. 'Thank you for coming, Mrs Stone. This is our little community.' She waved a plump arm at the scene.

She seated Doris in the picnic area of her tiny garden, saying that she would just pop in and make a cup of tea.

This gave Doris the opportunity to sit at ease and gaze around, to drink in the sweet air, to listen to the birdsong and to feel such peace as she had not known for years.

The dog wandered over to her and settled near. She became aware that one or two faces were looking briefly through lace curtains.

Mrs Williamson came out with the tea. 'They will want to see you, Mrs Stone. In case you choose to live here. And I hope you will. Because we are a very happy little community. We all look out for each other, so it's important who comes here.'

At that, a large cat jumped on to Doris' lap.

'Push him off, Mrs Stone. It's Fred, he's a bit too affectionate, always wants to sit on a knee. I hope he finds one when I'm gone.'

'Where are you going, Mrs Williamson?'

'I'm going to Australia to be near my son and see something of my grandchildren. Otherwise I wouldn't dream of leaving this place. Here's Mrs Johnson coming to say hello.'

'Hello,' said Mrs Johnson. She smiled and held out a plate with a few home-made buns. 'I made these for you to have with your cuppa. Janet told me you were coming to view today. So this is to say welcome.'

Doris could hardly speak. Tears stung her eyes and her lips felt uncertain. She was not used to kindness and it was not easy to bear.

Someone waved from the far corner.

'That's Marion,' Mrs Johnson said. 'She's got MS. I'll just go and help her into her chair. We all look after Marion you know, Mrs Stone. We're all her carers. Can you stand that?'

'I'd love to be of help, along with all of you,' said Doris, and felt she belonged, an emotion strange to her.

They went on a tour of the little home, Mrs Williamson explaining the running of the place.

Doris loved everything about it. The pink roses on the bedroom wall, especially. 'I used to have that paper in my room,' she exclaimed. 'Until I went all modern and fashionable. But that's gone now, it's all over, and this is a new beginning for me.'

They sat in the garden again and discussed it. Mrs Williamson hoped she would buy it and rather nervously said, 'Thirty thousand pounds?'

'Yes, yes,' said Doris.

'As a matter of fact, something I haven't mentioned, Mrs Stone, but the van next door belongs to me as well. I have been letting it for a little income. I don't suppose you would want to consider buying the two for, say, fifty thousand?' Mrs Williamson had dared to say this because she had noticed the diamonds on Mrs Stone's chubby fingers.

It all fell into place in Doris's head, like a predestined pattern, like a chunky wooden toy. As if it had all been there in her head for ever, as if it were part of her life plan and this was one of the final pieces to make the plaything work. Of course, she would buy the second caravan as well.

❀

'It's a lovely place, Mrs Traviss. It's got all fields around it. Like being in the countryside. There's a little shop on the corner and a bus that stops there and it takes you to more shops and a library. Once a week it goes to the market in Epping. And the people who live there are lovely. There's a retired couple called Mr and Mrs Johnson, an invalid lady called Marion. There's a man who works the forest, and a young couple with a baby, and some horses in the field next door, and . . . oh, I don't know, they all speak to you. They don't look right through you, they're friendly. I'll have to get used to it, Mrs Traviss. It's like a dream really. I can't wait to be sitting there with the cat on my knee and the rain hammering on the roof all cosy, like.' Doris collapsed to take a breath. She looked up over the ladies' underwear. 'What d'you think Mrs Traviss?'

'It's Shangri La, Mrs Stone. It's Shangri La.

Doris staggered from the emporium into the shabby street and leaned against the window, laughing with joy. Joy with herself that she hadn't told the whole tale. She had not mentioned the second caravan.

❁

Mr Day smiled. 'You have done very well, Mrs Stone,' he said. 'I feel you are going to be very happy there. You have kept everything within your means and even have a little bit left.'

'And a small rent, Mr Day.'

'A small rent, Mrs Stone, from the second caravan, for treats, no doubt, when you go into Epping market. But . . .' And here, Mr Day looked down and shifted his papers. 'But,' he began again, 'I suppose you should have some collateral to raise money, if need be. Have you, have you some little possessions which might be worth anything?'

Doris blushed. 'Er, well.'

'I knew Frankie well, Mrs Stone. He had exquisite taste in everything.'

Doris blushed again.

'I know he loved buying you gifts. And they would be the finest. Jewellery, for instance?' Mr Day raised his eyebrows. 'Diamonds?' he said.

'Lots of diamonds,' smiled Doris.

'Lots?'

'A big box full. They're all quite safe and all mine!'

'I knew Frankie wouldn't let you down, Doris.' Mr Day relaxed, smiling broadly. 'If you ever fancy a cruise

Doris

or anything extravagant and you wish to sell any of the pieces, I can get you the best price for them. Don't go to a dealer, will you?'

'I won't, Mr Day. I'll take care.'

⚜

Doris left her house without a backward glance. Mr Clark packed the taxi with her few possessions. She had left the cupboards spilling out with a mountain of clothes for Ophelia to sort out. She had a bag of wigs and a few things to start her wardrobe. She was looking forward to buying more in the market.

She carried her handbag, her jewel box and a paper carrier bag with the two photographs in their silver frames. She hugged them to her and stepped into the taxi.

Some weeks later, Doris was feeding a carrot to the pony in the next field. She kept glancing down the lane. The birds were singing and all was well with the world.

She was restless and couldn't help pacing around the gap in the hedge. And there it was. The chug, chug, chug of an ancient motor. Down the lane at a royal pace came Mr Clark. Stopping on the dot. He got out and opened the door for his passenger.

Doris stepped forward to greet her. 'Welcome home, Mrs Traviss. Welcome home.'

The Chemist

Notting Hill, 1946

Out of our house, down Ledbury Road and into Westbourne Grove, was the abode of Mr Bennett. The chemist.

It was more than a shop. It was his home which he loved with a passion and refused to spend a single night away from.

He stood there, benign and reassuring against the background of his paraphernalia – on the top shelf were the huge great green and blue bottles of his trade.

I remember one of my early moments with him was to show him a hurt to my hand which had turned nasty and was hot and swollen with pus.

He bent over the injured finger, then looked up and said, 'Go home, and do some washing. Have the water as hot as you can bear and keep your hands down into the clothes.'

The Chemist. 1946

Of course, it worked. Nowadays, some indifferent person would hand you an expensive tube of something and look at you as if they had never seen you before.

He told me a little of his early days when he was a young apprentice at the turn of the century. He worked in an industrial area and one of his main jobs was to dispense laudanum to the young mothers. These young women had to work very long hours in the factories for a mere pittance, having to leave their babies alone in some hovel in order to survive.

They had no choice but to dope them with laudanum, put them in a drawer – for they could not afford a cot – to sleep a drugged sleep. Then the mother would return, shake the child awake enough to take food, then dose it again with laudanum so that she might sleep to get up at an unearthly hour to return to some hellish factory. So the tedious process began again.

Some things are better now.